THE DANCING LADY

THE NINTH DAY

MIMI MILAN

EATON HOUSE

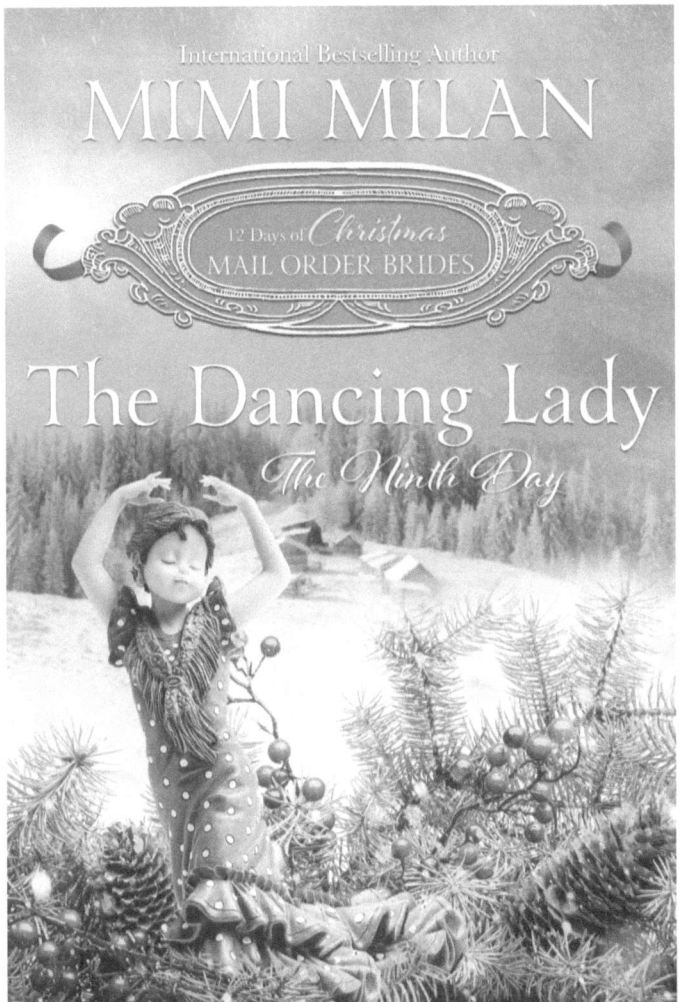

International Bestselling Author

MIMI MILAN

12 Days of *Christmas*
MAIL ORDER BRIDES

The Dancing Lady
The Ninth Day

The Twelve Days of Christmas
Mail Order Bride Series

The Dancing Lady

© 2017 by Michele Claudio

Cover design by EDH Graphics

❀ Created with Vellum

PRAISE FOR MIMI MILAN

What others are saying about Mimi Milan's books:

"I thoroughly enjoyed A Rebel in Jericho. *I felt that it was a great read. The plot was interesting and kept me turning the pages to find out what would happen next. The characters were well developed and interesting. I enjoyed the historical apsect and the description at the end of real events hinted at in the story. I like that the ending lends itself well to a sequel while effectively completing this story. I can't wait to read more by this author.*

I love that 20 percent of the sales from this book goes toward stopping human trafficking which is a bigger problem than we realize."

~ Carrie, Reader ~

*"*A Rebel in Jericho *has a little of everything for its readers to enjoy. Suspense, romance, deception, and the desire to survive. Catalina has an incredible strength within herself, while at the same time showing just how vulnerable she is. I was intrigued to find out what twist and turns would take place next with every page I turned. I look forward to continuing reading this series and what other adventures are to come."*

~ Warrior Ground ~

"This novel [Twice Redeemed] *touches on human trafficking and tugs on the human heart. The author, Mimi Milan, is a master storyteller. She invites the reader into her fictional story world set in Mexico and drops them into the scene of action. The reader experiences the story as if they are an observer watching the story of Jericho unfold. As they turn each page, the readers become invested in the plot, grow fond of the good characters, want to silence the bad guys and care deeply about how the story ends.*

The author drives the characterization deep and paints a picture on every page. The descriptions of each setting are vivid and believable. The dialogue is engaging and fresh. The plot thickens with the turn of each page and the theme of God's grace moves forward this story of redemption.

I believe that this story is worth every bit of a five-star rating. It's worthy of winning a literary award."

~ Writer at Heart ~

"I really enjoyed all three of the novellas in this series (the Angel Paws Rescue series). *Each novella is surprisingly very different from the other, but each has a wounded veteran and an arts person as the hero and heroine with a pet/service animal adopted from Angel Paws Rescue. I recommend the series to anyone who enjoys clean, heart-warming contemporary romance."*

~ MH, Reader ~

ACKNOWLEDGMENTS

I always like to take a moment in the beginning of any novel and thank those who came together to help me produce it. So, please excuse me if I gush over a couple of tried and true individuals. Amongst them would be, first and foremost, the Master Creator and Original Storyteller, without whom this series would have never come to be. I thank Him for walking with me every step of the way, but most of all for giving me the gift of stories. Without them, I would be lost.

To my wonderful editor, Patricia Highton, you truly are the grammar girl extraordinaire. Eaton House has been made all the better because of your expertise and attention to detail. (By the way, I *do* know what ellipses are for. I just can't help myself.)

I also wish to show my appreciation for the family and friends who continue to show me support by continuing to read and provide useful feedback.

To the cover artist for this particular project, Erin of EDH Graphics, thank you for creating such a timeless cover.

To my husband, you get all my heartfelt gratitude once again for supporting me in a career that doesn't quite pay the bills as well as it feeds the soul. Your never-ending support and encouragement are inspiring.

Finally, I deeply appreciate all the readers out there who offer their support and allow me to entertain them with my books. I write these stories for you. May they continue to amuse, inform and inspire.

CHAPTER 1

 *oelle, Colorado*
December 24, 1876

JOSEFINA WAS GOING to scream if she had to listen to one more complaint – especially from that Maybelle woman who was traveling with them. *Santa Maria!* The way the woman went on, you would have thought she was as entitled as she suggested instead of being stuck on this wagon like everyone else. Not that she really knew her story. She didn't know – or care to know – any of the other brides Mrs. Genevieve Walters had procured for the men of Noelle. Although, maybe that wasn't the right attitude to have about the entire affair. After all, some of the women seemed extremely kind and even generous with one another. She wondered if the same could be said about the man she was contracted to marry. He was asking a lot more of her than she could really give. The fault was more hers than his, though. She was the one who had lied her way into the group. Not that she had really *wanted* to be married. However, it seemed like the best solution at the time.

But could she pull off the charade of being a domesticated woman?

She pulled out the letter the intended groom had sent only a few months prior and read it again.

DEAR JOSEFINA MORALES DE ZAPATERO,

OJALÁ QUE TODO VAYA BIEN. I must admit that I am doing quite well myself – especially since receiving your letter. Rather, the letter Mrs. Walters of the Benevolent Society of Lost Lambs sent in your stead. It brings me great peace of mind to know that I have been blessed to find a woman with such wonderful qualities. When Mrs. Walters revealed that you are a God-fearing woman who can both cook and sew, I knew that it was no accident that our paths crossed. Perhaps you'll find this a little bold, or maybe not since you are of such strong faith, but surely la Virgen has brought us together. What other explanation could there be of two Mexican Americans finding each other through a matchmaking service?

Now, I honestly cannot boast about having any great skill or talent. At least not like you. I most certainly cannot stitch together fine articles of clothing, let alone something as intriguing as dancing shoes. However, I do enjoy dancing itself and while not the most graceful, I am certainly pleased to learn that it is a pastime we will be able to share together. In fact, I even have a guitar that I enjoy strumming now and then. It is only a little fun, but perhaps we can find a useful song or two.

Of course, I do not want to leave you with the thought that I have absolutely nothing more to offer. When you arrive in our fine town, you will see first-hand how the name of Villanueva is one of protection and prosperity. As the proprietor of a newly established restaurant, you will see that there is no finer dining anywhere in town. Together, working side by side to create dishes that can be savored by aroma alone, we can make Nacho's Tacos even better. Yes, food is my greatest passion. It is a joy to know you feel likewise.

I look forward to cooking up a wonderful future together. Until we meet, todo mi respecto y más.

Sinceramente,

Ignacio Villanueva

JOSEFINA NEATLY FOLDED THE LETTER. Glancing around to be sure no one was watching, she once again tucked it back into the safe space between her plump bosoms. Well, safe now that she was out of Denver and far from Hank's Whisky River saloon. She could still kick herself for getting involved with the man and his horrid business to begin with. Why hadn't she been smart enough to realize his idea of "dancing" was not the traditional steps her mother had taught her? Not that her mother had been any kind of saint herself.

A small frown tugged at the corners of her mouth when she thought of the matriarch and her dastardly attempt to sell Josefina's "flower" at the innocent age of seventeen. Thankfully, neither the buyer nor her mother could nego-tiate what either felt was a fair price and the deal fell through. However, the damage had been done. Shock turned into dismay which then rolled into bitter waves of distrust. Angry, she waited until her mother fell asleep one evening and swiped all the cash the two of them had earned from their performances, or rather, from Josefina's performances. After a nasty fall from a horse, her mother became more of a manager than a dancer. She booked performances in any place that would pay. From nice establishments to seedy saloons, they traveled all over the countryside together.

It was a shame her mother had grown so greedy. It was equally terrible that Josefina had reacted so harshly. Striking out on her own, she hadn't half the connections her mother did. She didn't have that winning personality to sell her performances either. It was too late to turn back, though. Word reached her several months after their parting that her mother had passed on.

Then came along Hank and his lies. Low on money and food, she had signed that contract without even reading it – not even realizing dancing was only one part of the requirements. Foolish girl! She did her best to not believe pretty words anymore. Not that she heard any other than the word "fina" when one of Hank's customers showed her interest. The only benefit of *that* arrangement was the choice of *who* she privately entertained and that half the take was hers. So she was usually fortunate enough to have someone relatively handsome who practiced at least some form of personal hygiene.

Was this Ignacio fellow handsome? If not, surely he was clean. After all, he worked in a kitchen.

She thought about the letter again.

Nachos Tacos. Food is my passion.

Forget that he knew a couple of little dance steps or liked to fiddle with a guitar for fun. He was probably like those fat, rich ejidatarios in Mexico – with lots of land and luck. That's what she was going to need if she was going to get her hand on enough money to find her father and sister.

Luck… to learn how to cook!

"I swear, my toes are going to fall off if we don't get there soon!" Maybelle grumbled again.

"Patience, ladies. We're almost there." The man driving the mule team (Woody, if Josefina recalled correctly) slapped the reins once more, urging the animals to pick up speed. He seemed nice enough, but she was glad she wasn't marrying *that* one. She couldn't imagine being stuck with a bunch of smelly beasts. Speaking of which...

She looked over at another bride-to-be in the group and shook her head. There sat Molly Norris with that wretched goose of hers, gently cradling it like a newborn child. Beside her was another who actually *did* have a child with her.

Santa Maria.

Josefina shook her head and mentally crossed herself. And here she was thinking she had problems. All she needed to do was learn how to cook. These women...

These women!

Why hadn't she thought of it before? Maybe being a little more sociable wasn't such a bad idea. If she befriended the other brides, then perhaps she could convince one or two of them to share their recipes with her. She would be cooking up mouthwatering meals at *Nacho's Tacos* in no time! Then she and this Nacho would say "I do" and her husband would be obligated to help find her family. No decent, self-respecting man would do less.

"Whoa," Woody called out to the mules as they finally descended upon the town and stopped out front of a building with a sign that read, *The Golden Nugget.* "Here we are, ladies. Just head on in so the Reverend can get to performing the weddings."

There was a gasp amongst the group, followed by a myriad of murmured questions.

"What did he say?"

"In the *saloon*?"

"How can he marry us in there?"

"I'm not saying 'I do' in front of a bottle of rotgut!"

Mrs. Walters waved her hands to get their attention. "Now, girls, don't worry. I'm sure there's a suitable explanation here," she turned towards the saloon door with a quiet growl rumbling from beneath her breath, "there better be."

Josefina frowned as she and the other women stumbled through the snow and into the saloon. Of all the places, why were they *here*? She didn't mind so much that the weddings weren't being held inside a church. But a saloon? It looked like she had escaped one – only to end up in another!

If one thing was for certain, though, they were about to find out what the men of Noelle were up to Mrs. Walters would see to that! She stormed ahead of the group, her entire form – from flashing eyes to heavy footfall – all full of fury. Her growing temper blazed in her green eyes as she approached a man dressed like clergy. "The esteemed Reverend Hammond, I presume?"

Josefina had to hand it to their custodian. The woman could remain completely poised while still thoroughly expressing her displeasure in such a manner that an individual would have to take leave of their mental faculties to cross her more than once. Why, Josefina remembered this one time in Denver when a man whistled at one of the girls while they were leaving.

"The nerve of that man!" Mrs. Walters rambled on about the benefits of horsewhipping the Reverend or some such. Josefina couldn't tell exactly, having been distracted by Molly who was desperately trying to keep her goose hidden.

"Afraid your friend might end up on the menu?" she teased the woman.

"Very funny, Fina." Molly rolled her eyes. "You know how he gets around new people. I don't want him thinking it's necessary to defend me if my intended tries to... well, you know, greet me with an embrace or something."

Josefina thought about her own intended and grimaced. She hadn't thought much about how they would greet each other. She scanned the room of men, trying to guess which one might be hers. So far, no one was coming forward to claim her. At least she hadn't suffered Felicity's fate, though. The groom had taken one look at her and hightailed it out of there. She looked over at the bride-*not*-to-be. She seemed lost in thought.

That one... always gathering the wool.

"Hey, nena." Josefina snapped her fingers in front of the Felicity's face. The woman jumped. "Looks like we're leaving."

Felicity mentioned something about strategizing instead of daydreaming. Josefina couldn't fault her for it. She was doing a bit of "strategizing" herself so she could get back to her father and sister.

She would rather do it in a place that was warm and cozy, though.

"Vamos," she urged the other women forward. The Reverend apparently had better quarters in mind than the saloon they were currently standing in, and she wanted to get there *fast!*

The women shuffled out and were once again out in the cold, but the wagons had already been put up. So, they steadily lumbered down the town's center street towards their new destination, the weight of the weather visibly affecting all of them. Josefina noted the women in the group. She had to admit that she admired several of them. That Minnie Gold for instance. For someone who spent her whole life as a poor orphan, serving her family as a maid, she appeared quite noble. The way she marched down the street, head held high as she braced the cold... Well, her fortitude was certainly something to respect.

Unlike Maybelle's disposition.

"Now we have to walk? I have never!"

Josefina had "never" either. As in she had never said anything too ugly to another woman. She didn't want to begin now, either. Ignoring the cantankerous bride as best she could, she turned her attention to the buildings that lined the streets. There were several she knew she would want to visit one day soon, but her main concern at the moment was the one that appeared to be *Nacho's Tacos*.

No puede ser.

Josefina couldn't believe the small log building was Señor Villanueva's restaurant.

"Fine dining indeed," she mumbled.

"What was that?" Her head snapped up to find Kezia Merga, a beautiful gypsy widow with a quizzical look on her face, gently rocking her baby hidden beneath a thick cloak.

"Nada," Josefina quickly muttered. Having to explain to her new groom why she came with a baby in tow, the woman was bound to have enough trouble. No reason to give her any more with petty gripes. A thought flashed in Josefina's mind, though. The woman had a child. Perhaps she knew her way around the home. If so, Josefina could offer to watch the child in exchange for a recipe or two. It was worth the consideration. She gave the woman a nod, her chin leading first. "You look... how can I say... *bien lista*. You know, like a worldly woman who might know a thing or two. Si?"

Kezia shrugged. Her face filled with hesitancy. She slowly responded, "I suppose it would depend on the heart of the matter."

"Didn't you work in a restaurant or something?" Josefina pressed. "You know how to cook, yes?"

"Actually, I washed dishes at a hotel restaurant."

Josefina deflated a little.

"I guess I learned a few things from watching the chefs, though. I bake an amazing apple pie... and no one in the state can touch my goulash. I'm fairly certain of that!"

The response earned the woman one of Josefina's brilliant smiles – the one she saved for people she actually liked. She got one in return and the women both fell silent as they marched on, their feet sinking in deep inches of snow. They were finally led to a large log building with a sign out front.

La Maison des Chats.

Josefina frowned. She didn't know much French, but she was fluent in Spanish and the similarities between the two were enough to make her question what kind of accommodations the Reverend had found for them. She shook her feet in an attempt to clear her boots of the cold snow that clung to them and she suddenly didn't care where they stayed. Compared to her native Mexico and her former Texas, this wintery weather was far from her liking. Any place was better than standing outside!

The Reverend excused himself to check out the place first and Josefina offered her opinion to a few of the other brides that maybe the place had rats. Although, she was fairly certain her idea of what hid within the building's four walls was somewhat different than what the others may have been thinking. Finally, the Reverend ushered them in.

She urged one of the women, a Chinese acrobat by the name of Meizhen, forward and then plowed onward with the rest of them, briefly noting what appeared to be a smashed lamp (or something else that could produce an equal number of glass shards) on the ground beside the door. It reminded her of the time she threw a prized vase at a belligerent drunk who refused to pay her after his... entertainment. While Hank had been less annoyed about the vase than he was about a customer double-crossing one of his girls, the cost of the broken heirloom had still been taken out of her pay.

"To appease my dearly departed grandmother's soul," Hank had joked. "May she rest in peace."

Now Josefina briefly wondered about the kind of altercation that could have led to this particular mess, but then she nimbly jetéd over it, her curiosity brushed away as she tumbled into the warmth the so-called mansion offered. A round of relieved sighs sounded from the entire group and even Mrs. Walters expressed her approval.

"Well at last..."

The Reverend began to show the women around when a nearly naked man shot down the stairs, past the girls and out the door... followed by another. Several of the ladies gasped. Josefina wanted to cackle like the bruja who used to prescribe her herbal teas for colds and other ailments. She may have had a greater gift for dance than healing and intuition, but anyone with two good eyes and some common sense would have known La Maison des Chats was not at all what it appeared to be.

Mrs. Walters demanded an explanation while a couple of the brides clear-away fainted. Josefina gathered up the few that seemed to have enough good sense to keep their heads straight and shooed them into the nearby parlor.

"I told you there were rats," she stated as a matter-of-fact. Her triumph was short-lived, though. Soon they were undergoing introductions with the Reverend (who flustered quite brilliantly to find Molly hiding a goose beneath her winter wear). Josefina stifled a laugh, until the Reverend turned his attention to her. Childhood days at Sunday misa came rushing back and she suddenly felt like a naughty child caught talking during prayer. She brazenly introduced herself, but was glad to escape down the hall with a handful of other girls, her nose following a delicious aroma that made her mouth water. She didn't make it to *La Maison's* kitchen, though. Instead, a young blond met them on the steps.

Josefina smiled at her when the woman, Pearl, amiably introduced herself. She had kindly put a soup on the stove to help warm the women up. Now she was offering to show them to their sleeping quarters.

"Just a minute!" Mrs. Walters grilled the young woman about her business in the building. Upon learning that Pearl was one of the whores employed there, the matchmaker gasped. A mutter of disgust escaped from under her breath. Pearl had the decorum to ignore the comment.

"Ladies? If you'll follow me," she graciously offered.

Josefina shrugged and quickly followed the woman. However, her mind reeled. If there was ever a time she wanted to snap at someone for being judgmental, now was the moment. How dare Genevieve Walters think less of someone simply because the woman had a less-than-desirable profession? It was the very reason Josefina had hidden her own dark past. Had the *Benevolent Society of Lost Lambs* known that Josefina was more than a dancing girl – that she had actually slept with some of the patrons – she would have never been taken on as a bride.

And with the way things were going, chances were good Mrs. Walters would still turn her out if she knew the truth.

Josefina kept her mouth shut even after they found themselves in their bedrooms. She was too busy listening to the commotion downstairs.

"That's Madame Bonheur," Pearl informed them about the proprietor of *La Maison des Chats*.

Shrieks sounded from the woman, followed by the sound of shattering glass and Mrs. Walters sobs of shock. The Reverend seemed stuck between trying to appease them both.

"Look, ladies. I'm hungry… and quite frankly, too curious to hide in a bedroom." Josefina excused herself and quickly descended the stairs despite the cries of protest. She ignored them, though. This Madame what-have-you seemed quite serious about her threats to make everyone "be sorry" they had displeased her. Josefina wasn't the sort to pursue trouble, but she definitely wanted to know what it looked like if it came seeking *her* out!

She tumbled into the hallway only to come face-to-face with the woman who had to be the "Madame" they heard screaming mere moments earlier. Stern and solid, the matron looked quite formidable. Eyes slit like razor-sharp knives, she raised a single, challenging brow.

Why, what an unpleasant… *cualquiera*. Was that supposed to scare her?

Josefina wanted to laugh. Head tilted to one side, she folded her arms across her chest and smiled as pleasantly as possible. The Madame hissed at her and Mrs. Walters quickly rushed to her side.

"Don't worry, dear. Everything is going to turn out swimmingly. Isn't it Reverend?"

"Of course," he quickly answered. The look he gave Madame Bonheur didn't go unnoticed. She growled at him one last time.

"Like I said, you'll pay for this."

She stormed off towards the door, stopping briefly when she noticed a framed plate hanging on the wall beside the entrance. It appeared to be the only one left that hadn't been smashed to smithereens. She neatly plucked it off the wall, spun around and flung it at them. The Reverend rushed forward to push both she and Mrs. Walters out of the way of the flying debris. It landed squarely in his arm before falling to the floor and shattering like all the others.

"Ow!"

Mrs. Walters rushed to the Reverend's aid. "Why, you—"

The door slammed solidly shut, cutting her off mid-sentence. Mrs. Walters stomped a foot and even raised a shaking fist in the air, earning Josefina's admiration with her spitfire display. The woman turned around and, seeing she had quite the audience, brushed her hands down her dress in an attempt to smooth it. She plastered on a smile.

"Come, dear." She wrapped an arm around Josefina and urged her forward. "Let's collect the others for dinner."

CHAPTER 2

N oelle, Colorado
December 25, 1876

IGNACIO COULD HAVE GIVEN himself a good, swift kick. All his planning to impress his bride-to-be and what happened? He didn't even make it to the alter.

A la Madre! He didn't even make it to "hello."

It was like one thing after another stood in his way of saying "Si, acepto" the day the women arrived. First, Jack Peregrine's grandfather, Gus, stopped in for a quick bite to eat – except he couldn't decide between bean burritos or bean soup. Then the poor viejo took twice as long to gum his food. Okay, maybe he had teeth…

But in that case, he needed to learn how to use them!

Who was he trying to fool, though? He could have boxed up the meal and asked Grandpa Gus to take his food to go. It wouldn't have been the first time the man had to hurry back to Jack's shipping shop before it was noticed he was missing. Not that it would have made things different for Ignacio.

Even after the man left, Nacho made more attempt at cleaning the restaurant than he did hurrying down to Seamus's bar. He kept trying to tell himself that it was because he wanted to present his señorita with as beautiful a business as possible – especially after exaggerating a bit on how grand his place was to begin with.

Okay, maybe he exaggerated more than a little.

He had big plans, though. So it really could be grand... with a little help. That's when it dawned on him that he was getting in his own way of achieving his dreams. He raced over to *The Golden Nugget* as quickly as his two feet could carry him. Of course, he couldn't go empty-handed. He wasted another ten minutes, looking around as he wondered what he could bring to present as a gift. Then he remembered the ribbon he had purchased a few years earlier for...

Ignacio shook the thought from his mind much like he'd done the night before when his memory had been tickled. It didn't really matter who the ribbon had originally been intended for, so long as it was never actually *given* to anyone else. The important thing was that it had never been worn in another's braid. Now *that* would have been a little tasteless and cheap. But facts being as they were, it should have made a fine gift to his new bride.

He fingered the turquoise satin once again. Slightly faded and unraveling at the ends, he had trimmed it a bit (another five minutes looking for a knife sharp enough to do the job right). Then he poured himself a cup of coffee... just to give himself enough time to consider the most appropriate way to present the ribbon. A thought popped into his head and he snapped his fingers. Draining the cup, he placed it on the counter with the rest of the dishes to be washed once he returned home with his bride.

It will be nice to have someone help clean this mess up, he thought as he wrapped two bean burritos in a cloth servieta and carefully tied the colorful ribbon around it.

"Eso es," he said to himself. "Now she will have a nice little something, but not so nice as to expect a life of luxury."

Unable to find any more reasons to stall, he made his way to *The Golden Nugget*.

"Ya just missed them, man."

"Como?" Ignacio slapped the food on the bar counter, upset that his bride must have been married off to someone else. "Tell me, Seamus, how is that even possible?"

Seamus gave him a questionable look. "Aw, Nacho, ya knew what time they were coming in. The Reverend had told ya the same as everyone else. So, don't try acting daft with me. It won't work. I know ya was getting the cold feet."

"I don't have cold feet," Ignacio protested. "I'm happy to get married."

Seamus's lips thinned, but he remained silent. Instead, he grabbed a mug and filled it with his best brew. He slid the cup in front of his friend and watched him drain it.

"That should put ya right for heading down to *La Masion des Chats*."

"What? Why would I need to go down there?"

"Because that's where the Reverend had the ladies relocated."

"Relocated?" Nacho was confused. "Why would they be relocated *there* after getting married? They should have gone to their new homes."

Seamus sighed. "Because they didn't git married... and they sure as hell-is-full-of-sinners weren't boarding up here."

Nacho shook his head, rattling his beer-soaked brain. "Wait a minute, amigo. Are you saying no one married my woman?"

A slow, thin smile lit up Seamus's face. "Ay, that's exactly what I've been telling ya. Yer wee woman is spending the night at Madame Bonheur's place – waiting for you to go pick her up and take her home."

Just the mention of the Madame's name made Nacho's stomach churn. If there was ever a woman he never again wanted to deal with...

"Well," he hesitated, "I think that calls for a drink."

Seamus frowned. "Are ya sure about that, man? After all, ya wouldn't want to be getting drunk *before* saying the vows."

Nacho frowned. "Come now, amigo. Have you ever known me to actually get drunk?"

"Well, there was that one time—"

"Funerals don't count," Nacho interrupted.

"No. I've never known ya to get drunk," Seamus reluctantly admitted.

"Well, then?" Nacho asked expectantly. He picked up the mug and waved it around until Seamus grabbed it. Seconds later and Nacho was forgetting all his troubles...

And his bride.

Now here he was the following morning, rushing around the diner once more, trying his hardest to push out the workers who kept stopping in for his *pan dulce* and *café con leche* before heading out to the mines. Some of them still believed they would find gold, but he had hung up his hat on that one. There was no time to chase after empty dreams of quick riches when he had a legitimate business to run.

Which was why he had to hurry up and claim his bride. He ran the risk of another hombre snatching her up with every passing minute. He let out a frustrated sigh and picked up one of his Talavera mugs. He tapped a fork against it – soft at first to avoid chipping the delicate pottery. When that failed to get everyone's attention, he loudly cleared his throat.

"Come on, everybody. You know I'm trying to get out of here."

"Where's the fire, Nacho?" One man joked.

"Yeah, there's plenty of *cold* around here to put it out," another added.

Peals of laughter sounded throughout the diner and he knew they were all having a good laugh on him for having been the first to volunteer for marriage... and the only one that failed to show up.

"Better hope she doesn't think you left her at the altar," the first man joked again and Nacho wanted to punch him in the nose. It would be just like Elmer Copperpot to put his two cents in where it didn't belong.

It would be just like him to go and steal Nacho's bride, too. Everyone had heard about his questionable dealings with a foreigner who had passed through town looking for work. Elmer had hired him to build his house. When the time came to compensate the man, he claimed the fella hadn't done a proper job and paid him far less than originally agreed upon. Of course, Nacho couldn't really say whether or not it was true. However, he had ridden a time or two past Elmer's place when going out to survey his own land. While he couldn't speak much to the interior, the house looked fairly sound from the outside. In fact, his casa looked bien bonita – pretty enough to entice almost any woman to marry the skinny weasel.

Nacho picked up a washcloth and wiped off a nearby table. "You're the last person I'd have to worry about anything from, Elmer," he grumbled and returned to his original post.

Orvis Weston, another miner who had been watching the merrymaking, came up to pay for his coffee. "Don't worry about them," he said as he slapped his money down on the counter. "They're just jealous they didn't draw any straws."

The laughter died down and a few of the men grumbled about rigged straws and such, but the suggestion sounded silly even to their own ears. Well, everyone except Elmer. He continued gripping about how one of those women should've belonged to him. Still, he lined up like the rest of the men. One by one, they paid their bills and shuffled out of the diner. Nacho walked around to a couple of the tables and picked up the mugs. Orvis followed him.

"Here, let me help you."

"Aw, gracias, amigo. You don't have to do that."

"I know I don't," Orvis said. "Just figured it would help you get on down to *La Maison* a bit faster. Besides, I was heading that way myself."

Nacho smiled. "Looking to see your lady friend, are you?"

Orvis grinned like a singing bird who had just heard his favorite tune. "You know it."

Nacho couldn't fault him for falling in love with one of the Madame's working girls. After all, he himself had done the same once.

He gave his head a shake. The last thing he wanted to do was think about *her* again – especially when he was trying to move on to a new chapter in his life. Instead, he focused at the task at hand. "Thanks for helping out, Orvis."

"Not a problem," his friend replied and the two men quickly worked at clearing off the rest of the tables. Orvis followed Nacho into the kitchen, an armful of plates and mugs weighing him down.

"Just leave them with the rest," Nacho instructed.

Orvis stared at the incredible pile. "Are you sure?"

"Yeah, it's fine. I'm going to have some help around here soon. Remember?"

His friend frowned. "You talking your gal? The one you plan on marrying?"

"Si, señor." Nacho grinned wildly. "That's exactly what I'm talking about. No more running around like a backwards

19

mule. I'm going to have someone to help cook *and* clean – a real domesticated lady."

"Sounds like you should've hired a servant instead," Orvis mumbled.

"Nah," Nacho said as he stacked his own set of dirty dishes with the rest of the pile. Then he stopped, one plate still held in midair. "That is what wives are for, no?"

Orvis shrugged. "Guess it depends on the wife. Don't forget, though, most women like to feel like they're someone special… and you haven't sealed the deal with yours just yet. Another hombre comes around, making her feel all important, and she could always change her mind."

Would she do that, Nacho wondered. Sure, it was possible. Orvis was technically right. They hadn't exchanged vows yet. However, they had reached an agreement. He would protect her and provide for her. In exchange, she would help him around the restaurant. He looked around the kitchen, taking in quick inventory. The pileta was piled high with dirty dishes, as was the counter space beside it. The table he used to prepare food still had scraps and dried, caked flour glued to it. The floors looked like they hadn't been swept in a good solid week. Nacho let out a tired sigh.

"Maybe you're right," he finally admitted to his friend. "Maybe I should clean up a little before bringing her back. You go on and see your gal."

"You sure? I could always stick around and sweep or something."

"No, no. Don't worry about it. I know you need to get up to the mine with the rest of the guys. Plus, you've got that stop to make at *La Maison*. Thanks for helping clear the tables, though."

"Well, alright then. If you think you're good. Just don't take too long now. You don't want to keep *your* lady friend awaiting with the likes of Elmer Copperpot hanging around these parts. Man's about as low as a snake's belly in a wagon rut."

"Eso es," Nacho agreed and picked up a wash cloth. He once again thought about the foreigner Elmer had duped. "Truer words were never spoken, my friend."

~

"MAYBE HE'S NEVER COMING," Maybelle sneered. "That would make *two* grooms that have run off."

The girl gave Felicity a haughty look before turning to Josefina to do the same. If ever there was a name Josefina wanted to sacrifice to La Muerte... well, she would never actually do something like that. Oooh, but that Maybelle sure could tempt los santos themselves – and all the rest of Heaven, too!

"I don't think that's much of a problem anymore," Josefina smirked. She gave Felicity a wink, knowing that the girl seemed to have found a new interest... or that interest had found *her*. It looked like she was about to become a bride after all. Wouldn't that make for a nice Christmas? Not that the holiday meant much to her anyway. It was nice and all, but she preferred to celebrate *El Día de Reyes* – the day when the three wise men actually brought gifts to the Christ child. It had been a long time since she had truly celebrated the holiday, though. All the way back to when she and her sister...

Josefina let out a sigh.

"You okay?"

She looked up into the concerned eyes of Avis, a bride equally private as herself but certainly much more reserved. "Sí, amiga. I'm fine," she gave the girl a broad smile, "especially after the recipes you gave me last night.

Disappointed that Mr. Villanueva had failed to show up,

Josefina moped around *La Maison* until Avis decided to comfort her. The two of them ended up discussing some of Avis's favorite recipes late into the night. Josefina was confident she could pull off the fried chicken Avis had shared with her, or maybe even the oatmeal cookies.

If there was ever an occasion to do so! Here it was midmorning on Christmas morning and still no sign of—

"Fina!" A call from downstairs came. Josefina quickly jumped off the bed she shared with Cara and raced past quiet Meizhen, only to slow at the top of the stairs. Penelope Jackson (the bride that seemed to have bad luck following her everywhere) stood at the bottom, calling up. "There's a certain gentleman here waiting to meet you. Would you like me to offer him some coffee or tea until you come down?"

"No!" Josefina quickly replied. The woman's expression fell. "What I meant to say is thank you, Penny. I would like to do that myself – if you don't mind. You know, to show that I have some sense of hospitality and will make a good hostess for his restaurant."

Penny visibly brightened. "Oh, that makes sense! Okay. I'll just tell him to wait in the parlor."

"Thank you. I'll be right down."

Josefina raced back into the room.

"You better hurry up, or you might not have a groom left. Not with *that one* around," Maybelle jeered.

Josefina checked her reflection in a small mirror affixed to a vanity table. She straightened her rebozo, ensuring the shawl covered her shoulders with her braid neatly hanging over one side. Satisfied that everything was in place, she turned and headed out of the room, pausing long enough to snap, "I'm sure that would just break your heart."

She didn't wait for a reply. Rushing down the stairs, she nearly barreled into a man standing nearby. She tripped, falling headfirst into him.

"Oh, how clumsy of me! I'm so sorry," she gushed. Burning with embarrassment, she could hardly bring herself to look at the man as he straightened her up. His hands lingered on her arms, but she could only stare at her feet. "I swear, I never fall."

"Yeah, that's my job," Penny muttered and then groaned. "Which is probably why it happened. My bad luck must be spreading."

"Nonsense, Chiquita. Remember what I told you," Josefina said. She had already given the woman a prayer card with La Virgen on one side and a sincere prayer on the other. She was positive the girl's fortune was sure to turn around soon.

A smiling Penny nodded and excused herself.

"I'm glad to see how kind you are to your friends," the man spoke. "It gives me great hope you will treat our customers accordingly."

Our customers?

Josefina slowly looked up. This could not be the Ignacio Villanueva who had written to her. Where an old, squat Mexican cook should have stood was in his place a sun-kissed man with long, sweeping lashes covering eyes the color of graying skies over sea green oceans. A good head and a half taller than her, he was broad-shouldered and with a firm chin and equally strong hands.

Hands that were still holding her after the near-fall.

Josefina quickly straightened up and his arms fell to his side. A coy smile tugged at her lips. "I'm sorry. I don't think we've been properly introduced, señor."

"Yes, of course, you are right. How rude of me. Ignacio Villanueva, at your service." This time he offered his hand, but when she took it, he quickly turned hers over and brought it to his lips. His full lips brushed her knuckles with

23

a gentle kiss and her breath caught. "But you may call me Nacho, señorita."

And you can call me anything you want... so long as you call me!

A voice cleared from behind her and she spied the matchmaker from the corner of her eye. Josefina snuffed out any idea of acting overly flirtatious with her intended groom. "Oh, Mrs. Walters. I didn't know you were here. Please, allow me to introduce Mr. Villanueva."

"A pleasure," Nacho said. The matchmaker excused herself, leaving them to get better acquainted. "And you must be Señorita Morales."

"No, actually. I mean, yes. It is all my name – Morales de Zapatero. However, if you are only going to rely on one, then it would be Zapatero."

Nacho looked confused. "You go by your mother's surname?"

"No. It belongs to my father."

"How strange."

Josefina bristled. Did he just call her... *strange*? She kept her temper in check, but couldn't refrain from tilting her pretty nose up. "I suppose no stranger than the name Villanueva being one of 'protection and prosperity.' Isn't that what you wrote in your letter?" she challenged.

"It *is* a name protection and prosperity," he insisted. Then he gave her a sheepish smile. "Just maybe not so much in the town of Noelle... yet. It will be, though. Soon, I will be as successful as all my brothers."

"Ah, so your brothers all know how to cook?"

"My brothers? Oh, no, señorita. They do not own restaurants. They are ranchers. In fact, they own one of the largest spreads in Texas."

So, he came from a wealthy family. That was something. Still, it didn't answer the question...

"Then it was your mother who taught you how to cook?"

Nacho hesitated. "Well, not exactly. You see, my mother was an excellent cook – that is where I got my passion for food. But my father? He thought I should be out learning how to do everything my brothers were learning. You know, to run the ranch so we would be prepared for when he passed it on to us. So, I didn't get to spend as much time as I would have liked in the kitchen."

Josefina contemplated what he revealed. Perhaps she wouldn't need to rely on any of the other women to teach her how to cook. If she could convince him to make a meal for her...

"Señor, I have to be honest. I understand the desire to want to do something. But to do it well? That takes practice. Sometimes many years."

She was thinking about her talents as a dancer. It wasn't something she learned overnight, but trained most her life to perfect – just as her mother before her and her grandmother before that. Of course, she couldn't reveal to him she was little more than a dancing girl.

A soiled one no less.

"Are you questioning my skills as a cook?" Nacho asked. He crossed his arms and took a stance that much reminded her of her own father. Full of bravado before he was certain to lose an argument. She smiled sweetly. The man was playing right into her plan.

"I don't mean to offend you, Señor Villanueva. However, you were the one who called *me* strange. Remember? I am just trying to point out that it is equally peculiar that a person should know how to cook – or even run a restaurant – when they had no one to learn these things from."

"I... Well..." Nacho struggled to formulate a logical response. He threw his hands up in surrender. An amused chuckle escaped. "Oye. Let's get something straight first, okay? Because I think maybe we are having a little misunderstanding. I was not calling you strange, amor. I would never do that. Before all else, I am a gentleman. So, I don't call beautiful women strange. *Entiendes?* I was simply trying to understand why your parents switched your name around. I mean, you have to admit... that is not very common in our culture. Yes?"

He was waiting for a response, but she was still stuck on the fact that he had called her "beautiful" and "amor" along with the *way* he had said those words. They held such conviction. No, Mr. Villanueva was nothing like the men she had entertained in Hank's saloon. Those men had been little more than demeaning animals. But *this* man? She couldn't even begin to imagine what life would be like to a man who spoke kindly to her. She couldn't even look to her own parents as an example of a good marriage. All the two had ever done was fight due to a combination of her father's lofty demands and her mother's stubbornness – a trait Josefina was guilty of herself. However, it certainly wasn't the way she wanted to present herself to her future husband.

She finally found her voice. "You are right. I am being difficult. You have my sincerest apologies."

Nacho waved away her confession. "It is okay. I too am nervous, señorita."

"Please, call me Josefina... or even Fina, if you'd prefer. I have gone by that for some time now."

"It is easy to see why. You are easily the finest woman I've ever had the privilege to meet."

Heat rushed to Josefina's cheeks. She modestly hung her head. "Señor Villanueva—"

"Please, call me Nacho." He placed a finger under her chin, encouraging her to look at him. "That is the best way to start things, no?"

"Yes, of course." Josefina nodded her agreement, but her excitement was short-lived.

"First names and fine food," Nacho continued.

"Fine food?"

"At *Nacho's Tacos*," he explained. "I closed the restaurant early so we could spend a little time together. It is Christmas, after all. I figured most everyone would be with their families, celebrating the holiday. We can do the same over at the diner."

"You celebrate Christmas?"

"Of course. Don't you?"

"Not really," she admitted. "Our day to celebrate the Christ child was *El Día de Reyes* on the sixth of every January."

"Ah, yes. Three Kings Day. We did that as well," Nacho explained. "You see, my father was Mexican. Hence, the last name 'Villanueva.' However, my mother was American."

She was surprised. "Your father married a white woman? Surely, her family protested."

"Well, they weren't too pleased from what I was told. However, they began to change their minds once the grandchildren started coming. Besides, my father was not the kind of man to be slighted. He worked hard, procured a lot of land and proved himself worthy by running one of the finest ranches in southern Texas... and that is what we are going to do."

"We are?"

Smiling, Nacho reached out and took hold of her hands. His eyes grew soft as he cradled them; his voice was a whisper. "Yes. The town of Noelle will know our restaurant to be the finest around when we prove ourselves to them. That is, of course, after we prove ourselves to each other. Sí?"

Prove themselves to each other? Oh, no. He expected her to cook... *NOW*. What could she possibly say to stall the inevitable moment of standing in his kitchen, trying to command a cast iron stove?

Standing in his kitchen? That's it!

Smiling, she politely pulled her hands from his and ignored the bereft feeling of his missing warmth. "Nacho, I cannot think of anything better that I would like to do than accompany you. However, you must understand that my reputation is at stake. It simply wouldn't be proper for the two of us to be alone in your restaurant."

Nacho sighed. "Of course, you are right. How foolish of me to even consider asking you to risk such a thing. We do not want the town to talk badly of you. That would be terrible for business."

She bit the inside of her lip, slightly irritated that he seemed more concerned about making his restaurant successful than he did for her good name. Not that she had much of one outside the town of Noelle anyway. Still, that wasn't something he knew anything about.

"I could go with you," a small voice offered.

Josefina twisted around to find Penny standing at the parlor entrance.

Oh, of all the people!

"That would be most kind of you, Señorita... I'm sorry. What is your name?"

"Penelope. Her name is Ms. Penelope Jackson," Josefina offered flatly. She had a good mind to remind the woman that there was a reason for the nickname "Bad Luck Penny." Not that she really thought the woman brought bad luck, but it was awfully unlucky that she would offer a way to leave right when Josefina was trying to avoid Nacho's restaurant.

"Señora Jackson, thank you so kindly. Fina and I are most appreciative of your gracious offer."

"Yes," Josefina found the urge to let out a long, frustrated sigh. Instead, she pasted on a smile. Although even she could feel that it died before reaching her eyes. "We're so pleased you'll be joining us for lunch. However, I forgot to mention that I must also watch Kezia's child this afternoon, little Jem. That way she can spend a little quality time with her beau. So, you understand why I must keep my word."

"I would never want you to break a promise. You have *my* word that I will have you back well before then."

"Very well," Josefina agreed. She turned to Penny who stood by, wringing her hands. "If you'll excuse us while we get our coats."

"Yes, good idea! I'll go prepare the wagon while you ladies get ready to go."

The two women watched him leave. As soon as the front door shut, Josefina whirled back to Penny. "Perdiste la mente? What were you thinking?!"

"I really didn't mean any harm," the woman bumbled. "I thought I was helping."

Josefina buried her head in her hands and moaned. "I know. It is I who should be sorry, Penny. It's not your fault I don't know how to cook."

"You don't know how to cook?" Penny asked.

"No," Josefina admitted. She grew serious, hardening a little. "And you're the only one I've told. So, you better not go spreading it around. *Sale?*"

"I would never," Penny promised. She crossed her heart. "Your secret is safe with me and – if you'd like – I'd even be happy to show you what I know when we get to the restaurant."

Josefina brightened, but quickly deflated again. It was Penny, after all. Bad luck seemed to follow her like stench on dead fish. "You still got that card I gave you?"

The woman nodded.

"You've been reciting the prayer on it?"

Penny hesitated. "A few times."

"Well, let's hope a few is good enough. Go grab your coat."

The woman did as requested. Josefina reached for the doorknob, but then stopped. "Wait a minute," she said. She turned Penny around. From forehead to navel and then horizontal, she crossed the girl. Then she spat over each shoulder.

"What in the world are you doing?" Penny questioned, a look of disgust crossing her face.

"Making sure the Devil doesn't follow. Now let's go, Chiquita. We've got a meal to make!"

CHAPTER 3

"It's wonderful that you have a wagon," Josefina said as they pulled up to the front of the restaurant.

"Thank you," Nacho replied and flared his chest.

Asi es, papacito. That's how you win the lady!

He dismounted and rushed around to her side to offer his hand. Josefina accepted it and carefully placed her foot on the wagon wheel.

"The horses are nice too," Penny chimed in.

No sooner had the words left her mouth, Josefina's foot slipped off the icy wheel. She tumbled forward, head first and with such surprise she didn't even have time to scream. Still, Nacho was quick to act. He swiftly wrapped his arms around her, bearing all her weight. They landed in the cold snow with a solid *THUD!* Nacho groaned.

"Ay, perdóname." Josefina tried to push herself up, but her foot slipped and she once again fell on him. Tears flooded her eyes. "I'm so sorry."

"I don't believe anything is broken," Nacho said with a

mischievous smile. "Besides, I would be in no hurry to get up if it weren't for the cold snow in my pants."

Josefina gasped. "Señor Villanueva!"

She playfully slapped his chest. He released her just enough to grab hold of her hand. He turned it over and placed a kiss in her palm.

"Eh hem."

They both looked up to find Penny had descended the wagon by herself. She stood over them, once again wringing her hands.

"I'm so sorry, Mr. Villanueva. I didn't mean to distract Fina." She turned to her friend. "Perhaps this wasn't such a good idea. Maybe I shouldn't have come."

"Nonsense." Josefina rolled off Nacho. They helped one another stand back up.

Penny leaned towards Josefina, her voice dropped low to a whisper. "I can see my bad luck's rubbing off on you."

Nacho let out a laugh. "There's no such thing as bad luck, Ms. Jackson. There's just lots of snow and ice!"

"He's right," Josefina agreed. They followed Nacho into the diner and she mumbled only loud enough for Penny to hear her. "It wasn't bad luck *this* time."

"Just don't say I didn't warn you," the woman replied as they entered the restaurant.

"So, what do you think?" Nacho made a sweeping motion. "Welcome to *Nacho's Tacos* – the finest dining in all of Noelle."

Josefina refrained from reminding him that it was the only dining establishment in the town. Luckily, so did her friend. They both looked around their surroundings. Josefina smiled pleasantly, appreciative of what she found. A long wooden table with benches for larger groups sat in the middle of the room. Along the walls were several smaller tables for more intimate dining.

"The kitchen is through here," Nacho offered.

Penny hung back. She slid off her coat and took a seat at one of the tables. "I think I'll stay right here while you go check it out, Josefina. It might be safer that way."

"Okay, nena. Don't forget what we talked about earlier, though." Josefina jerked her head in the direction of the kitchen.

"I won't," Penny promised.

"What was that all about?" Nacho asked as they passed through the swinging door leading into the kitchen.

"Nothing special." Josefina waved away his question. "The girl showed some interest in learning how to make Mexican food for when she marries. I told her I would show her what I know."

"Well, don't show her too much. I wouldn't want to lose any business."

"No, of course not." Josefina contemplated his words for a moment. "Although, it would be easier to avoid sharing any special recipes you want to keep secret if you tell me what they are."

"I can do even better than that. It's already past the lunch hour. I can make them for you and you and Ms. Jackson can enjoy some of my fine cooking."

"Really? You would do that for us?"

If smiles could win awards, Nacho would have taken first place with the one he gave her. He beamed brightly. "For you, señorita, I would do anything."

A delicious shiver ran up Josefina's spine. She wasn't normally the giggling type, but if this *pedacito de pastel* continued speaking so sweetly, then she was going to come wholly undone! Most of her experience had been with men who insulted her with their expectations that payment for pleasure included the lewdest license imaginable. Her intended's attempts of winning her affections were far more romantic.

She glanced away, bashful. "Please, Nacho, you're going to make me forget that I'm a lady."

"My apologies," he said. "You're right. I have taken far too many liberties." He bent his head in an effort to meet her gaze. When she finally looked up, he continued. "I am not too proud to admit, though, that I am trying my hardest to win your heart."

Josefina swallowed against the firm lump forming in her throat. She felt like such a fraud. Here was a man truly interested in winning her affections and what was she doing? Planning on using him to get back to her father and sister. She hung her head again. "Nacho—"

"Not another word, mi serenita. I will be on my best behavior from here on out," he promised. "For now, we cook! If you'll allow me?"

He helped her slip out of her coat and hung it on a hook near the door. Then he deftly moved around her and pulled the lid off a pot already sitting on the cast iron stove.

"What have you there?" she asked.

"Beans that I left to soak overnight. They should be ready for the olla de frijoles now." He grabbed an iron to stoke the warm embers that remained from breakfast. "The stove should not take too long to heat. It's still warm from the *pan* I baked earlier today."

"What kind of *pan* do you like to make?"

"I know how to make anything from *puerquitos* to *orejas*, but my favorite of all are *conchas*."

The sound of soft white bread baked in a decorative shell of sugar made her stomach rumble. Nacho laughed.

"I know that sound! Better go ahead and throw in some salt."

"Throw in some salt?"

"Of course." He grimaced. "You don't try to eat your beans without it, do you?"

"No, never." Josefina looked around and grabbed a bowl of white granules. She began to pour it into the pot.

"No!"

Startled, she jumped and even more dropped in. He grabbed the vessel out of her hand.

"I'm sorry," she said.

He let out a slow sigh.

"It isn't your fault. I don't have any of the bowls labeled and you are new to this kitchen. How were you to know which was the sugar?" He placed the dish back on the prepping table and reached for the smaller one beside it. He handed it to her along with a spoon. "I tend to use less salt than sugar, so I keep it in the smaller bowl."

Josefina nodded and scooped a single spoon out. She slowly sprinkled it into the pot, hesitating while she thought of the best way to figure out how much salt he liked in his food. "Each cook has their own taste. I wouldn't want to make it too salty."

"You're right," he said. "I don't think that would be possible with the sugar we just added, though. So, put in however much you think it will take to balance it out while I begin the eggs."

"Eggs?" Josefina scrunched her nose up.

"Of course," Nacho looked at her curiously, "for the *huevos y frijoles*."

"Oh, yes. But of course."

Josefina's mind raced. She could slightly recall after her mother ran off and her father took over the cooking. He made the same meal for her and her younger sister, Elena. But then their mother returned to claim Josefina and now her mind was filled with ten years of American cooking. She had seen so many different meals in places all throughout the

United States. Images from fried chicken to leftover scraps crammed her mind, making it impossible to recall the recipe of such a simple dish like eggs and beans. Were the eggs fried or scrambled? Were the beans whole or smashed? She couldn't remember.

Slowly adding in one more ladle of salt, she carefully glanced his way. He was cracking the eggs open and dropping them in a bowl.

"So, you like your eggs scrambled?" she ventured.

"Not particularly. Why do you?"

She shrugged and placed the salt bowl down. "Not particularly."

"Oh." Strained silence fell between them. Nacho finally spoke again. "Then why did you ask?"

"I saw you putting all the eggs into the bowl. I thought you were going to scramble them."

"No, I just like to pour them in the pan all at once. That way they cook evenly and are easier for me to separate and flip."

She looked for something more to say. "Well, that is different."

His hand paused over the bowl. "It is?"

"Sure," she continued. "I would think that you would just cook one at a time."

He poured the eggs into the heated pan and set the bowl down on the table. Chuckling, he grabbed a cloth and wiped his hands. "Oh, I forgot. You are used to cooking in the home where things are nice and peaceful. You will see it is much different in a restaurant. Sometimes there are so many orders, it's hard to keep up."

She frowned. "It is?"

He placed his hands on her shoulders and gave them a gentle squeeze. "Do not worry, Fina. You are strong and smart. Just cook the same you would at home and I'm sure everything will turn out fine. You'll see."

"I'm sure you're right," she said.

He gave her arm a reassuring pat just as the kitchen door swung open. Penny stuck her head in. "I hate to bother the two of you, but a guest arrived."

"Guest?" They chorused.

"Yes. It's that doctor fellow."

"Ay." Nacho slapped his forehead. "I forgot to lock the front door after we came in."

"We can just tell him we're closed," Josefina suggested.

"Most certainly not," Nacho replied. "Doctor Deane is one of my best customers. He eats many meals here. We cannot turn him away."

"No, I suppose we can't."

"That's my girl," Nacho cheered. He turned to Penny. "Didn't you say you wanted to help out?"

The woman hesitated. "Um… yes."

"Great! Then you can set the tables." He turned to Josefina and explained, "I just got new settings. I wanted you to see that the business is doing well. So, I had some Talavera shipped in."

Josefina's mind immediately raced back to her childhood once again, and she almost admitted that it had been a long time since she'd seen the delicate pottery bless any tabletop. "I'm sure they're beautiful."

"Would you like to see them?"

She nodded.

"Okay. Follow me." He stopped and turned back to Penny. "Ms. Jackson, could you please see to it that our guests are seated? Then you can come back for the drinks while Fina and I get the plates and finish the cooking."

"That should be safe," Penny smiled and scampered back off to the dining room.

"This way," Nacho motioned to Josefina. He pulled out a set of keys from his pocket and unlocked a door off the side of the kitchen. "This leads to the apartment I keep in town."

"You live in town?"

"For the most part," he said and fell strangely quiet.

She followed him down a short corridor and into the apartment, noting that it was nothing more than a one-room setup with meager furnishings. A bed was in one corner of the room with a small nightstand beside it, positioned under a single draped window that provided the entirety of lighting. In the opposite corner was a modest, slightly decorative three panel dressing screen. A picnic scene in a charming pink decoupage enhanced the dark cherry oak that framed it.

She might not have understood much French, but she did know French things when she saw them. The fact that he could have ordered such a beautiful object in such a short period of time meant one of two things. Either he was a very wealthy man who could command immediate gratification... or the folding screen had already been in his possession.

"It's quite beautiful."

"Oh, it's nothing really." Clearing his throat, he further explained. "It is just meant to hide the chamber pot and bathing tub."

She looked around the room once more and noted that there was no indoor plumbing. Having been at Hank's for so long, she had come to take such a thing for granted. Now she was aware of the slight inconvenience. Still, that didn't satisfy her curiosity.

"When did you come into possession of—"

"Do you smell that?"

Nacho sniffed the air. Josefina looked up to see smoke filtering into the room.

The eggs.

"Dios mio!" Nacho yelled. He ran out of the room, down

the corridor and back into the kitchen with Josefina right behind him. Penny stood over the burnt eggs, waving a cloth over them.

"Oh, this is all my fault," she said. "This would have never happened if I hadn't gotten caught up talking to Doctor Deane. I should've came back for the plates sooner."

"Nonsense," Josefina said. Although, she herself inwardly questioned if it could have been another case of bad luck. First there was the fall from the wagon. Now this?

Nacho found another cloth and grabbed the cast iron handle. He carried the entire thing to the back door and opened it wide. He tossed the eggs out and they landed on the snow-covered ground, the cold sizzling beneath them.

"Fina's right," he said. He swung the door back and forth several times to try to air the room out faster. "This is my fault. I have so much on my mind that I forgot to remove the eggs before I left the room. I should have never left the stove unattended. That isn't bad luck, but proof that anyone can make a mistake."

"If you say so," Penny conceded. Still, the woman looked utterly dejected.

"We do," Josefina smiled. She turned to Nacho and gently laid a hand on his arm, halting him in mid-action from fanning out the smoke. She softly said, "I don't think it's a good idea for us to be in here right now."

"A little smoke never hurt anyone."

She inwardly groaned. The point was that she didn't want to be the next one to burn something – which was bound to happen if she had to produce some more eggs. After what had happened with the beans, it was almost a guarantee she would make another mistake. She pasted on yet another smile as she chided him. "Nacho, amor, it is not the smoke that concerns me as much as it is my friend. Clearly you can see that she blames herself for this incident. I know that you wouldn't want any future customer to be saddened while in your restaurant, though. It would leave a bad taste in their mouth, no?"

Nacho took her words into consideration. "You are right, of course. Please, take Ms. Jackson to the dining room and give her one of the tables near the window. They are the best in the house. Also, a cup of café or tea to settle her nerves – whichever she prefers, naturally."

"Of course," Josefina agreed. "I will also take the Talavera and set the tables myself."

"Yes, that will work very nice. Thank you."

"Come, Penny." She escorted the bride back to the dining area where she found that the doctor had claimed one of the good tables Nacho had mentioned. She wondered if he had intentions to see Cara, the Irish beauty that was part of their group. Although, if she thought about it carefully, Cara hadn't looked too pleased the first time she saw the good doctor.

"Doctor Deane." She nodded to him as she showed Penny to the table opposite where he sat. "I will return in one moment with your plate."

She excused herself and rushed back to the kitchen, past Nacho and into the apartment. Then she popped out once again, a set of dishes in her hands.

"Bring them here and I'll fill them," Nacho instructed.

"Why not just bring the pot out to the dining room? Then I can serve everyone at the same time without having to run back and forth to the kitchen."

"Good thinking, wif—"

His mouth clamed shut when he realized what he had nearly said. He grew quiet. "I am terribly sorry."

"Why apologize? It is normal when one feels like they've fallen into a routine with someone. Besides, isn't that why I'm here – to be your wife?"

"Yes," he replied. One strong hand reached out and fingered the long braid hanging loosely over her shoulder. "And you will make the most beautiful bride."

Surprisingly out of character, Josefina blushed furiously. She glanced away. "You have quite the golden tongue, señor."

"No, I only speak the truth. You honestly are the most beautiful woman I've known. From the way you care about how your friend fares to the other you've agreed to help this evening with her child... Well, it's easy for a man to have a golden tongue when the woman he plans to court has such a golden heart."

He dug into his pocket then and produced a small paper package. *"Tenga.* I wanted to give this to you yesterday, but I wasn't able to make it out of the diner as I had hoped. When I did, it was already kind of late and I got caught up talking to Seamus."

She placed the plates on the table beside her and accepted the small parcel. "Ay, Nacho. You didn't have to do that."

"I know, but I wanted to."

She slowly unwrapped the package. Inside was the prettiest turquoise ribbon she had ever seen.

"It's exquisite," she exclaimed. "Now I feel bad that I didn't get you anything."

He shrugged as if he hadn't expected anything in return. "No te preocupes. Are you sure you like it?"

She nodded. "Very much. I shall tie it in my braid."

"That will look lovely," he said and she laced the ribbon around her plaited tress, tying a bow at the end of the tail.

"Now I will take the plates out to the dining room and see what our guests have to say about your lovely gift. You finish up the meal and bring it out as soon as you can. Sí?"

"Asi es," he agreed and watched with great satisfaction as she sauntered out of the kitchen, a stack of plates in her hands and a smile on her face.

This was the kind of relationship he had hoped for when he first married...

Colette.

An image of his deceased wife flashed in his mind. *No*, he scolded himself. This was nothing at all like Colette. She had been nothing more than...

A whore.

He cringed at the word – hated using it. It wasn't the profession itself that he was against. God and Madame Bonheur only knew how many times he had visited the place over the past few years. The problem he had was that he had fallen in love with one of her women and then made the terrible mistake of marrying her. Oh, he had tried – Dios and all the santos knew how hard he worked to make her an honest woman. The moment she told him she was pregnant, he whisked her away in the dark of night from *La Maison* and right to the Reverend. By moonlight he married them, summer sweltering over the couple like their unfurled passion. He could still remember repeatedly wiping his sweaty hands against his trousers as he vowed to love and honor Colette all the days of their lives.

He just hadn't realized her life would have been so short-lived.

"We are closed!"

A shout from the dining room snapped him out of his reverie. He scurried out of the kitchen only to find his worst nightmare standing in the opened entrance. He composed himself, standing as tall as possible.

"My dear Nacho!" Madame Bonheur oozed false pleasantries. "I must say, you would do well to teach your new... friend... how to greet paying customers. Never have I felt so unwelcomed."

"Good afternoon, Madame Bonheur." Nacho gave her a courteous nod. He glanced over at Josefina to find her standing there with one hand on the doorknob and the other formed into a tight fist planted firmly on her hip. A menacing scowl marred her pretty face as she refused to let the Madame enter. Nacho couldn't blame her, but knew he had to appease the old bird if he was ever going to have any peace in his life. "I'm sorry you have felt unwelcomed, Señora. However, Ms. Zapatero is correct in stating that we are closed today. I'm sure you understand. After all, it is Christmas."

"That's precisely why I've come!" The woman pushed past the infuriated Josefina and rushed up to Nacho, her face the look of feigned concern. "Why, if I recall correctly, it was this time last year that our dear Colette passed. Isn't that right?"

Nacho looked up at Josefina to find she had stilled, her formerly passionate countenance now an expressionless one. He swallowed hard and turned back to Madame Bonheur. "Señora, I believe you are gravely mistaken."

"Mistaken?" The woman let out a chilling laugh. "Dear, how could you have possibly forgotten your poor wife? I most certainly haven't. After all, it was I whom you stole her from. Remember?"

At the sound of the word "wife," the other two women had expressed their shock. However, the only one that really registered was Josefina's cry of indignation. This time Nacho refused to look at her, though. Instead, he stared down Madame Bonheur. He bit back a growl rumbling dangerously from the back of his throat. "What I meant, Señora, is that you are mistaken regarding *when* she passed. It has been two long years now. Therefore, your concern is not needed."

The woman waved away his words. "Oh, my heavens. For me to forget when it occurred. I suppose that must be a sign of old age setting in, or perhaps the sadness of the season. After all, she was such a joy to us all. I know you certainly enjoyed her. Yes, Nacho?"

It didn't go unnoticed by any of them how Madame Bonheur stressed the word "enjoy" and he noted the wicked gleam that shone in the woman's eyes.

"Yes, well, now there will be reason to rejoice once again. No?" Josefina slammed the door shut and strode to Nacho's side. She gave the woman a look of superiority and then nodded at him. "Didn't your letter say something about owning a guitar?"

A corner of Nacho's mouth turned up. "Yes."

"Well, hombre? Do you still have it?

"Actually, yes. I store it under the bed."

"Antos, traelo. You promised me a song. Remember?"

"It's been a minute since I've played, but if you will grab the pot and serve up the frijoles then I will go tune the guitar. *De acuerdo?"*

"Agreed."

She hurried off towards the kitchen. Once she disappeared, Nacho gave Madame Bonheur his undivided attention again. Ignoring the curious looks from his other customers, he leaned close to her and lowered his voice. "Señora, I will remind you kindly that this is not *La Maison.* This is *my* place of business. You are more than welcomed to stay provided you remember that."

The woman's lips curved into a nasty smirk. "Of course, Señor Villanueva."

She saw herself to a table just as Josefina returned with the frijoles. "Where is the guitar?"

"I'm getting it right now," he said and disappeared from the room.

Josefina made her way to the first table. She set down a plate of bread and then dished out a hearty spoonful of beans onto Doctor Deane's plate.

"I've heard tell that you are an incredible dancer," he said.

Josefina had the decency to remain humble. "I suppose I know a step or two."

"She's just being modest," Penny spoke up from across the way. "I've seen her when she's thought no one was looking. She's quite spirited."

"Qué preciosa. You are too kind." Josefina beamed at her as she finished serving the doctor. "We are out of eggs, but I'm sure you'll love our beans. They were made special today."

"Thank you," he said. "They certainly smell enticing."

Josefina only nodded and moved on to Penny. She spoke quietly. "Hey, chica. I'm going to give you some of these beans, but I'm not so sure you're going to like them."

"Why not?"

"I had a little accident and poured a bunch of sugar in the pot."

Penny's eyes grew wide. "If I had followed through on my promise to teach you how to cook—"

"Nena, don't worry yourself. I wasn't trying to say you're to blame. I was just warning you so you don't get the... well, you know..." Josefina motioned to her stomach, "*chorro*."

A look of confusion crossed her friend's face and then her eyes widened once more. "Oh." She looked at the doctor already eating his meal. "Oh, no."

"Don't worry. I gave him a bunch of bread. Now I have to serve *la dragona*."

The words "dragon lady" made Penny laughed. However, she quickly quieted when she saw the Madame raise a questioning brow her way. "You're bad, Fina."

"Only sometimes," her friend stated matter-of-fact and then made her way to the dreadful woman sitting at a dark corner table. Josefina could only imagine how the woman enjoyed sitting there, the dim shadows providing her coverage so she could better study the rest of them. She approached the woman and plopped the pot of beans down on the table.

"Buen provecho," she said with an eager grin.

"Excusez moi?"

"Oh, there's no need. I have more class than that."

"No need for what?" the Madame snapped, her French accent sliding into something a little more familiar – similar to that which Josefina had heard the night before when the woman argued with Genevieve and the Reverend.

"There's no need to beg," Josefina explained. "I forgive you."

The Madame's teeth could be heard grinding inside her head. "I wasn't asking for your forgiveness. I don't need it. What is the meaning of *this*?"

The woman pointed to the pot.

"Oh, I'm terribly sorry. You are right. It is *I* who must ask your forgiveness. You see, I have been so busy with my… how do you say? *Prometido*? That's right. Fiancé. But you already know that seeing as it is as French as are you." Josefina gave her a challenging glare.

"Get to the point," Madame Bonheur barked.

"Well, as I was saying, we have been so incredibly busy that I didn't have time to wash all the plates. Seeing as they are all dirty, this is all we can offer you at the time."

Madame Bonheur's glare slowly changed into a look of amusement. She shrugged. "Well, it is to be expected. Not all women can be as… capable… as was our lovely Colette."

Josefina's hand began to raise and she would have surely brought it squarely down on the wicked hag if Nacho hadn't walked through the door right then. She quickly spun towards him. "Please move the table and benches back and begin playing – something with a nice rise and fall that starts slow, builds and then ends dramatically. Can you do that?"

Nacho's mouth hung open with surprise. He slapped it shut. "I think so."

"Good. You do all that and I'll be right back. Don't wait for me, though. Just start playing."

He nodded and she rushed back into the kitchen where he had hung her coat. She quickly tied the rebozo around her waist, the embroidered shawl seductively hanging from her round hips. Then, digging into one of the coat's pockets, she pulled out a pair of castanets. She had just positioned the concave wooden shells in her hand, anchoring them into her palms with string tied around each, when she heard the strumming of Nacho's guitar. Head downward as if studying the floor, she slowly pushed through the door. She dragged one foot forward and then slapped it down. She repeated the movement with the other foot – each stomp keeping with the slow rhythm of the guitar. Then she dramatically looked up at the audience, captive in their seats. She turned sharply. Backs facing them, she slowly bent backwards, her arms sweeping over her head. She began snapping the castanets, shimmying her shoulders as she slowly straightened up again, her feet keeping with the same rhythm while she swung her hips from one side to the other. She performed several pirouettes, spinning around the room, never missing a beat.

Nacho watched, gripping desire growing with every move she made. The flick of her hand, snap of her skirt... He could hardly remember what he was playing – only that the Mexican ballad was not one normally paired with the flamenco. Yet she perfectly matched her movements to the music. Not that he knew much about the dance nor the level of difficulty involved. It was quite unlike the traditional Mexican dances like the Jarabe, and certainly much different from the ritualistic ones like the Concheros. It was similar and yet unique both at the same time – a fact he first realized when he had seen it during his travel from Texas. It could be mistaken for no other, and even Fina's stylistic flare was quite similar to the woman who…

The memory that flashed through his mind distracted him and then several things happened all at once. His fingers fumbled over the strings, missing several notes. Doctor Deane checked his watch. Madame Bonheur signaled for Penny. The woman stood to attend her and…

Josefina fell forward.

She didn't dare catch herself with her hands and risk cracking the precious castanets. Despite the bad blood that had existed between mother and daughter, they were the only things she had left to remember the woman by. Besides, good castanets were hard to come by. So as swiftly as she could, she drew her leg in close to her body, hoping to land on her foot. Unfortunately, the landing wasn't at all solid. The heel of her black leather shoe slid, twisting her foot sideways.

"Ow!" Josefina cried out and landed with a thud. "My foot."

Ignacio jumped up, but the guitar slowed him down and Doctor Deane arrived at Josefina's side first. "Let me take a look at that."

Carefully feeling along the bones of her foot, he asked her to move her foot side to side and then to flex them. She groaned in agony.

"Is she all right?" Nacho asked, his voice laced with concern.

"She'll be fine. It's just a sprain," the doctor said. He gave Josefina a stern shake of his finger. "Although, no more dancing for you, miss."

Josefina gasped. "No more dancing?"

"Not for the next few days at least," he clarified. "You need to remain off this foot if you wish it to heal properly. Once it does, you should be good as new."

"Is there anything I can do to help it heal faster?" she asked as both the doctor and Ignacio helped her stand.

"Well, a little snow wouldn't hurt," Doctor Deane said as he released her into Nacho's capable arms. "It would help take the swelling down a lot faster."

"I'll go get some," Penny offered. The woman's eyes glossed over and she hung her head with a distraught lament. "It's the least I can do."

"Penny, you don't think—"

The "bad luck bride" didn't wait to hear Josefina out. Instead, she abruptly raced out of the restaurant in search of the promised snow.

"Perhaps I should talk to her," Doctor Deane offered. He dug around in one of his pockets and pulled out a few dollars. "I was about to head out anyway. Thanks for letting me in on your day off. I believe this should cover the bill."

Nacho waved his hand away. "I couldn't possibly take your money. For the assistance you offered, such simple fare is hardly enough to repay you."

"Alright," Doctor Deane agreed. "Will you be on regular hours tomorrow?"

"Yes, of course."

"Then save my seat," the doctor said and tipped his hat at Josefina. "It was a lovely dance, by the way. Stay off that foot and get plenty of rest so we can catch another performance soon."

Josefina bowed graciously. "With more time to prepare, I promise it will be spectacular."

The doctor bid farewell as Penny entered again. He tried to speak to her, but she rushed right past him. Softened snow ran down her reddened hands and dripped water all over the floor. "I got the snow."

"I'll get a cloth," Nacho said. He helped Josefina sit in one of the chairs and made his way towards the kitchen. The door had barely swung closed when he reappeared holding a *servieta* normally reserved to keep the tortillas warm. Penny placed the melting mess onto the scarf and he bent low to place it on Josefina's ankle.

"How does that feel?"

"A little better."

"Good. Let's give it a few minutes and then I'll help get you in bed."

A cry of surprise sounded from the dark corner where Madame Bonheur still sat, an unassuming mask painting her face. "My dear Nacho, do you really think that wise? It could possibly set every tongue in town wagging – making her no better than Colette. Not that anyone could ever compare to our departed darling. *Oui?*"

"No, I suppose you're right in some small sense." Nacho turned to the woman who was quickly capturing his heart. "I'll go fetch your coat as well as make a little something for you to eat once you've returned to *La Maison.*"

He once again left the room, leaving the three women to weigh one another. Penny still looked remorseful that yet another day of bad dealings had followed her. She separated herself as far as possible from Josefina for fear that she'd bring her friend more bad luck.

Madame Bonheur, on the other hand, looked much happier than she did the evening before. Gone was *la dragona* who had threatened the Reverend and Genevieve Walters. A new target in sight, she turned a sickly-sweet smile onto Josefina.

"You'll have to excuse me if I don't wait to see you safely to my home. I have other matters to attend to. Speaking of which," she motioned to the pot of food still sitting on the table, "I am providing just as valuable a service as the good doctor. I'll not pay for such a miserable meal after being run out of my own dwelling. Now I must be off, but I did want to wish you luck, *Mademoiselle*."

Josefina held her head high. "Gracias, but I don't need any."

"Oh, I most certainly think you do. You see, I remember several years back that Liam Fulton had a ribbon very similar to that one in his store. I remembered it because I thought it was such a peculiar color and he must have traded the Utes for it." The Madame contemplated the idea and mumbled, "or perhaps he traded with Storm who usually trades with them?" She waved the idea away. "Well, it isn't important *how* it appeared in the store. What is important was how I wanted to buy it, but Liam refused to sell to me since it was already promised to another. So, it disappeared and I never saw it again... until now."

Why is this woman telling me all this?

Josefina rolled her eyes. "What is your point? You want my ribbon?"

A terrific smirk turned up the corners of Madame's mouth. "Really, girl, can you be so naive to not realize you're wearing a secondhand gift? Can you be so silly to not see that it belonged to another?"

The suggestion turned Josefina's blood as cold as the snow on her ankle. Could it be true? Had Nacho given her a gift that belonged to his deceased wife? A wife, by the way, he never even mentioned he had?

The sound of the front door snapping shut brought her back to the reality that she was sitting in the middle of a diner, nothing more than a damaged dancer who had become the understudy of a deceased wife.

CHAPTER 4

$\mathscr{N}$acho solemnly climbed back into his wagon, still disturbed by how quiet Josefina had been on the return ride to *La Maison*. At first, he thought it must have been due to the injury. She was obviously upset from the pain and didn't wish to speak. However, then they arrived at the cathouse and he saw the way she greeted the other brides – especially the gypsy woman, Kezia, and her infant daughter. The way Josefina showered the child with besitos softened his heart, but confused him further as to why she had acted so coldly towards him when he returned from the kitchen with her coat.

Not to mention the rest of the afternoon!

She had been sullen at best.

He slapped the reigns once again. What in the world could he have done to earn her disproval? If there was anyone who should have felt slighted, it was him. A sneaking suspicion made him question if she was being completely forthright with him about her past.

What are you talking about, old man? You don't know what her past is! All you know is that she is a woman who enjoys dancing and cooking and is interested in a husband who likes the same.

He shook his head. Who was he to question anyone anyway? It wasn't like he had been completely candid himself. Not that he had lied or anything. Surely, hearing that he had a wife was a surprise.

That's it!

Nacho slapped his forehead. How could he be so dense? She was upset because he had been married before. Not that he could completely understand *why* it would bother her. She had taken it with stride when Madame Bonheur mentioned it. In fact, she even boasted about there being joy in Nacho's life once again. Perhaps she had only been pretending it didn't bother her, and now she expected something to show his devotion to her. Yes, that had to be it.

He rode past the diner, deciding it would be best to keep the horses in the livery for the time being. The snowstorm may have blown over, but the weather was still biting cold. He arrived at the building a few minutes later and dismounted.

"Hola, amigo!" he greeted Culver Daniels. At more than six feet, Culver towered over Nacho (as well as most others in town). Still, he had to be one of the friendliest men Nacho ever met. "I'm glad I caught you. I was hoping I could put Jose and Maria up for the night. It's cold out there. Plus, Jose broke free from his post again."

"You still sleeping at the diner, Nacho?"

"Yeah, I figure it's easier that way. No travel to worry about. Just get up, roll out of bed and get to work. Maybe I'll start spending more time out at the homestead when I marry," Nacho's voice dropped to a mumble. "That's to say, *if* I marry."

"Well, you're lucky you caught me. I was getting ready to head on out." Culver said and approached one of the horses.

He ran a large, gentle hand down the horse's side. "You misbehaving again, Jose?"

Nacho laughed. "I can't seem to keep him away from Maria. That's why I thought I'd bring him down here. Maybe I can separate the two and he'll cool off. Although, maybe there's no hope with so much love in the air."

"I suppose you could say that."

"But would *you* say that, amigo?"

There was a small smile on Culver's face, but he fell silent. Nacho couldn't help but rib him a little. "Come on. Tell old Nacho. How are things going between you and your lady friend? It's the one with the baby, yes?"

"Yeah, that's her." Culver led the horse to an empty stall. "Actually, that's why I said you were lucky to catch me. I was only stopping by to check on things. I plan on going to talk to her after I leave."

"Far be it for me to get in your way, friend."

"Nah, you're not in my way." The man closed the door to the stall. "How are things going between you and the one you picked? Don't think I didn't notice that little 'if I get married' comment earlier."

Nacho shrugged. "I don't know. Things seem to be blowing a little hot and then cold again."

"That doesn't sound right. Not for a guy like you," Culver joked.

"I know. I don't know what I'm doing wrong. Everything seemed to be going so well. Now she seems upset with me. I have a sneaking suspicion as to why, but there's nothing I can do about it."

"Well, why do you think it is?"

"Because I was married to Colette."

Culver grunted. "Hmm. That doesn't sound right. Anyone's got to figure that we've all got a past – the women as well as the men."

54

Nacho thought about the woman Culver had been paired with. She came with an infant in tow. Yet, things seem to be sailing along rather smoothly for them. At least, as far as he knew… and certainly more so than it was for Nacho.

"You're right. I should just sit down and have a talk with her – explain why I didn't mention it before. Maybe that will smooth things over for us."

"Sounds like a good idea," the gentle giant gave Nacho a solid pat on the back. "Now, I hate to kick you out, but—"

"Don't worry, I understand. Go see your lady friend." Nacho made a slow walk for the livery door. "It's getting on to dinner time anyway. The restaurant might be closed, but I'll still need to cook for myself. I'll come by in the morning to check on the horses. Might go ahead and take them out again since Josefina injured her foot."

"She did?"

"Asi es," Nacho confirmed. "A peculiar thing the way she fell. She was dancing and… well, I don't know. It looked like that woman, Penelope Jackson, caused it. I'm not so sure, though. The look on Madame Bonheur's face…"

"Madame Bonheur? She was there?"

"Oh, yes. She came to see how I was faring – so she says – from losing Colette."

Culver's eyes grew wide. "I don't know what to tell you, Nacho. It sounds like she's still got it out for you."

"I think you might be right – especially seeing as to how Fina learned about my previous marriage because of the Madame's visit."

Culver let out a low whistle. "I don't want to say I told you so…"

"Ya sé, ya sé. I should have listened to you when you tried to warn me about falling for Colette to begin with. I won't make that mistake again. From now on, it's the straight and narrow for me."

The conversation trailed off and Nacho sighed. The last thing he wanted to think about was his dead wife. Thinking of her made him think of *other* things – like the reason he had married her to begin with.

He ran a hand through his hair and placed his hat back on. "Well, I better head out and let you do the same."

"Alright, Nacho. Let me know if you need anything. Have a good night."

Nacho threw his hand up in a lazy wave and shuffled out of the livery, walking back up the road, towards the diner. He gave some serious thought to stopping by Seamus's saloon again, but thought it best to just go on to the diner.

The last thing he expected was to find the door wide open, though! Nacho looked around but didn't see anyone. Either everyone was off trying to woo one of the new brides, or they were already celebrating Christmas with their families and friends.

So, who could have possibly been out in this cold… and seeking shelter in his restaurant?

His mind immediately raced to all the possibilities and one outweighed all the others.

A thief!

Nacho suddenly wished he had some kind of protection on him. Unfortunately, he had left it sitting behind the counter in the diner. He reasoned that everyone in Noelle had always gotten along relatively fine. Sure, there were fights now and then. Someone would have too much to drink and start a fight – accuse another of cheating at the card table. Noelle wasn't a dangerous town, though. Besides, they had Sheriff Draven in case things got a little too rowdy. So, no need to carry a gun on his hip.

Now he was thinking a little differently. What if some out-of-towner had followed the women into Noelle? What if they were the sort to shoot an unarmed man at first sight?

Alright. Maybe that first bit was a little farfetched. The rest was a real possibility, though.

He slowly approached the diner. Thankful the drapes had been drawn back for the day, he peered into one of the windows. The place was darker than usual, but the light from outside shone in just enough to show that it was empty. He advanced towards the door, quietly pushing it open.

"Hellooo."

He crept along the dining room, carefully stepping over the annoying boards that always creaked and made his way to the counter. He reached behind it, his fingers brushing against the pistol. At the same moment, the kitchen door violently swung open.

"Hey!" Nacho yanked the gun up to eye level.

"Blast this confounded contraption!" Grandpa Gus shook a coffee percolator in front of him. "How am I supposed to work this thing?"

"Gus?" Nacho stared at him, dumbfounded. "What are you doing here?"

"What am I doing here?" The elderly man asked. "What are you doing *there*, waving a gun around? Put that thing down before you hurt yourself."

Nacho immediately lowered the gun. "My apologies, señor. I didn't mean to frighten you."

"You didn't frighten me," the cantankerous man groused. "In fact, the only thing that frightens me is this... this... thing!"

He ferociously waved the metal pot again, the lid flipping back and forth with such force that Nacho was sure it would break at the hinge. He quickly replaced the gun back to its place and rushed over to Gus, grabbing the percolator from him before any real damage could be done. "Gus, does Jack know you're out right now? I would hate to think you wandered off again. You know how that makes him worry."

Thoroughly chided, the man looked away for a moment and Nacho knew the answer. He felt sorry for both men and hoped Jack would marry soon. It had to be difficult trying to run a business while caring for his senile grandfather.

"Well, I didn't ask for him or anyone else to worry about me," Gus groused. "I'm a grown man. I don't need a care-taker. However, what I could use is a good cup of that café you like to make every morning. Been having a hankering for it ever since I left the diner. Besides, it's the least you could offer after I came all this way to bring your Christmas gift."

Nacho ignored the fact that "all this way" was all of maybe a ten-minute walk and turned instead to the square package Gus pointed at. It sat at the edge of one of the tables. Large and squared and wrapped up in brown paper, Nacho picked it up and gave it a shake. His mind first wondered if it could have been from Fina, but he quickly dismissed the thought, reasoning that she would have simply brought it with her to the diner... and the likelihood that she would send it after the cold farewell he received was slim at best.

He flipped the package over and noticed a return address. *Home.*

Rather, what had been home once upon a time. He tenta-tively tore open the brown paper, wondering what his brother could possibly be sending him. The last communica-tion he had received was earlier that year when he learned his mother had fallen gravely ill. Nacho had rushed back to his childhood home, but it was too late. He stayed only long enough for the funeral and then returned to Noelle as fast as he could, burying himself in work once he arrived.

Removing the last of the paper, he found a box. On top was a letter which promptly fell out. He flipped it open and, finding a neatly penned message signed by his brother, couldn't help but wonder who had really written it. Two things he knew about Carlos was that the man struggled with reading and had atrocious penmanship. He pushed the thought aside, though, quickly scanning the note to learn that his mother's will had bequeathed to him her wedding band and beloved book of recipes.

"Ay, caray!"

Nacho dropped the letter to the table and ripped open the box. Tied to a piece of string wrapped around the book was a gold band. Set in the middle was a small, round garnet. He untied the ring and kissed it with reverence – the same traditional act performed every time he would visit his mother after a long spell away, bowing before fully embracing her. He stared at the ring a moment longer before pocketing it to focus on the book once again. Running a hand down the distressed brown leather, he slowly opened the cover and read the inscription inside.

> *To my beloved Ignacio,*
> *a child after my own heart*
> *who understands the importance of good food.*
> *Make me proud, hijo.*

"Anything good in there?"

Nacho looked up from the book to find Gus still waiting.

"Anything that might get me a cup of coffee?" the man asked again.

Standing, Nacho closed the book and tucked it under his arm. He smiled at the elderly gent. "Most certainly, amigo. It's the least I can do after you have traveled out in the cold to bring me such fine treasure."

"That good, is it?" The man raised a suspicious brow.

"Wouldn't happen to have enough gold in that box to save the town, would it?"

"I'm afraid not, my friend. That's why the men are getting married. Remember?"

"Yeah, I remember. I've got to get me one of those ladies. Gotta' figure out a plan."

Nacho only shook his head and lead Gus to a table. There was no explaining that only twelve men had been chosen for the mail order brides, and that the poor guy didn't stand a chance. "Well, while you give that some thought, I'll go ahead and get you a little something."

He returned to the kitchen, snatching up the percolator in one hand while the other held his mother's beloved recipes. He set the book on the table and the pot on the stove, ready to make the café con leche when a thought struck him.

What could be better on this chilly winter day than a nice, hot cup of atole?

The only problem was that attempts at making the beverage never turned out right. Whether it was an issue with the consistency or simply the taste itself, he could never replicate the delicious beverage of sweetened cornmeal. That is, it never turned out nearly as good as his mother had made for him as a child.

Nacho abandoned the coffeepot and flipped open the book, hopeful that a recipe waited inside. To his satisfaction, he found what he was looking for after a few pages. He ticked off the ingredients one by one.

Masa, sugar, chocolate, canela, water, milk...

Milk!

The item took him by surprise and he wondered if that was what had been missing all along. There was only one way to find out. Working his way around the kitchen, he found one dry good after another and set each on his prepping table. Then he went outside to the metal icebox he had commissioned Culver to create for storing cold foods. It had seemed funny to a few at first, but quickly proved preferable to the newer ones that utilized toxic liquid gases. Provided he packed enough snow and ice, the foods stayed cold just as well but without the added risk of accidental leakage of undesirable fumes.

Inside, he heated up some water on the wood burning stove. As he waited for it to come to a rumbling boil, he shaved a small bar of chocolate and measured out both the cornmeal and sugar. At the appropriate time, he poured all of them into the water, one by one, continually stirring until each dissolved. As the mixture cooked, he added in two cinnamon sticks.

The kitchen door opened.

"Did you fall into the pot?"

Nacho chuckled. "Ya, viejo. I was just about to bring this out. I wanted to make sure it was nice and thick before I did."

"Nice and thick? I like my coffee strong, but not so much as to walk on its own. Why did you thicken it?"

The question prompted another laugh. "I didn't make coffee this time. I tried something new that I'm sure you're going to love."

"New?" A worried look crossed Gus's face. "Aw, Nacho. Have ya lost yer mind? The whole town knows what happens when ya try something 'new.' I don't wanna be the first to test it out."

"Calm down, Gus… and wipe that look off your face. I'm about to serve you the finest beverage ever conceived – even better than that rot gut Seamus likes to sell. I'm sure you're going to love it. In fact, I'll let you eat here for a whole week – FREE – if you don't."

"I better like it," Gus quipped. He accepted the Talavera mug Nacho offered. "If I end up at Doc Deane's, then you're footing the bill."

Nacho raised his hands in defeat, silently agreeing to the man's demand, and watched as Gus took the first sip. The old man's face lit up with delight.

"Say! That's mighty fine." He took another, longer drink. After swallowing, he licked his lips and let out a sigh of satisfaction. "Mighty fine indeed. What did you say this was?"

"It's *atole*," Nacho explained. "This one is made with chocolate."

Gus chuckled. "Oooh, wee! You're gonna make a killing off of selling this stuff right here, Nacho. People will be draining their piggy banks for a taste of this."

Pleased, Nacho found a lid for the pot and covered it. "I hope you're right, amigo."

"I know I am," Gus said and drained the rest of his cup. He slapped it down on the table. "Say, why don't you give me another one to go. Then take some of that down to *La Maison* and ask yer gal if she don't think the same way I do about yer mama's recipe."

Nacho hesitated. "I don't know."

"Why not? Yer not getting cold feet, are you?"

"Funny you should use those words," Nacho mumbled. He grabbed a ladle and served the man another cup of atole.

"Oh, Lord. What's going on?" Gus asked as he eagerly accepted his second serving.

"I think *she* might be the one getting cold feet," Nacho explained.

"Well, maybe you ain't romancing her the way you should."

Offended, Nacho snorted.

"Stop making that noise. Ya ain't a horse," Gus snapped. "Now you just listen to old Grandpa Gus, ya hear? There's a little something you youngins seem to forget. Most men fall in love with their bellies, but a woman's way is straight to the heart. You understand what I'm saying?"

Nacho smiled, ignoring the elderly gent's mixed up sayings. "I think I understand. It is like my father used to say... 'A woman is like untouched soil. She grows what you sow.'"

"Exactly," Gus nodded. "High time you start listening to yer pa's words of wisdom."

There wasn't much that Nacho and his father had seen eye to eye on, but he couldn't recall a time his mother was ever unhappy. Perhaps his old man had gotten a few things right after all.

"Maybe you're right, Gus. I'll try to do as you suggest – possibly even take some atole to her tomorrow morning."

"So long as you're back here in enough time for the morning rush." The man finished off the rest of the chocolatey drink. "I plan on stopping by and getting me some more, too."

"Then I'll be sure to make extra," Nacho said as he walked the man out. He waved goodbye from the front entrance. "Thanks again, Gus."

He shut the door and bolted it (a rare practice) so that no other unexpected guests showed up, interrupting his study of the age-old family recipes his mother had handed down to him. As he flipped through the pages, he couldn't help but wonder what Josefina would think of the book. Would she be delighted to learn his mother's recipes, or would she consider the mention of yet another woman much like his ex-wife... an unwanted ghost from the past?

CHAPTER 5

oelle, Colorado
December 26, 1876

FINA BOUNCED the baby on one knee.

"I would be delighted to watch her," she exclaimed and buried her face under Jem's chin. She made small smacking noises until the baby squealed with delight. "Ay, tan preciosa. I could eat you up. Yes, I could. Yes, I could."

Zee laughed. "Thank you, Fina. Culver and I really appreciate the time alone. We'll be back this afternoon for her."

"Not a problem," Fina said. "I don't have any intentions of going anywhere."

She meant ever word, too. Despite forgiving the fact that Nacho had gifted her a present that had belonged to his dead wife, she was in no position to go anywhere. The swelling around her ankle had reduced considerably thanks to all the snow she had packed on it the day before. The prayer card of the Virgen of Guadalupe stuffed in her shoe didn't bring any harm either. Still, neither treatment had been enough to set her right again. She could barely hobble around the house, let alone take a walk down to the diner. So, she was more than happy to watch the baby as Zee and Culver celebrated their wedding.

She waved the bride off and focused on the baby again when one of Madame's girls, Angelique, shuffled by. Head down, it was obvious the girl was trying to go unnoticed.

"Oye, nena. You looking for Avis?"

The young woman looked up and silently nodded. Fina's heart immediately went out to her. She had heard about the girl's inability to speak and suspected that she had been poorly treated. Of course, there was no saying for sure. She felt bad for her, though. Her dark hair, slight figure and sad eyes reminded Fina of her own sister, Elena, on the last day the two saw each other. Elena had fallen to her knees, pleading that her sister stay with her and papa. All Fina could think of was that her mother had finally returned and had promised to take her on the greatest adventure of her life.

Had someone made Angelique that promise, too?

Fina thumbed to the stairs. "I can't say for certain, but you could always try upstairs."

Angelique gave her a thankful smile and nodded before leaving the room.

"And what about us, amor?" Fina asked the baby and bounced her yet again. She had gotten a late start to the day, barely eating breakfast as she worried about whether or not she had ruined her chances with Nacho. However, now she could feel the rumblings of hunger gnawing at the pit of her stomach. She stroked the child's cheek. "Do you think we should find a few scraps to eat?"

"Scraps?" The sound of shock and indignation made her swivel in her seat. "Señorita, surely you joke."

The sight of Nacho standing before her made Fina warm. "Señor, I did not expect to find you here."

"And why not?" Nacho asked. "When I bid you goodbye yesterday, did I not say I would see you again?"

"Yes, you did." Fina looked down, pretending to preoccupy herself with the baby. She straightened the child's outfit and then jiggled her up and down a few times. "I was afraid you had changed your mind, though."

Nacho took a seat across from her. "Why did you think that?"

Embarrassed, she avoided his eyes until the last possible moment.

"My behavior was less than exemplary yesterday." She glanced into his dark eyes, noticing that they looked as troubled as she felt. "Can you forgive me?"

"There is nothing to forgive, but I have to confess that I was at a bit of a loss yesterday. Things were going so well earlier in the day." He hesitated and pointed to her ankle. "Perhaps not *so* very well with the injury you suffered, but before that. We were cooking, you were dancing... and then nothing. It was like the weather. One minute, nice. The next minute, a sudden snowstorm blows in and leaves everything like ice. Tell me, Josefina. What happened? Did I say something to upset you?"

Fina let out a tired sigh. So, he had no idea of what was wrong. She shifted the baby to one side and reached into a pocket to produce the beautiful ribbon Nacho had given her the previous day. "I'm sorry, Ignacio. My behavior was uncalled for. However, I'm sure you will understand that I couldn't possibly accept a gift that belonged to your wife – especially not something as personal as the ribbons she wore in her hair."

Looking away, she held the turquoise strip to him, hopeful he would understand. The very thought that she had wrapped the same string after it had been in his lover's hair made her shiver with disgust. She could almost imagine

Nacho running a hand down some phantom woman's braid, his fingers trailing through her hair only to pull on the ribbon until it came undone. Then they would tumble out of sight, into some tryst too intimate – and too painful – for even her active mind to conjure up. The very thought brought a lump to her throat. Her eyes began to burn. Her voice quivered when she finally spoke again.

"Don't you think anymore of me than that?

Nacho stood and walked over to her, gently accepting the ribbon as he knelt down in front of her chair.

"You're right. It was thoughtless of me to give you something that had been intended for another. I simply didn't want to arrive to our first meeting emptyhanded, and it was the first thing that came to mind. I realize now that it was reckless. Had I considered it better, I'm sure I could have come up with something much more suitable." He grasped her free hand in earnest, the other still wrapped around the child who precociously sat in the crook of Fina's arm, trying hard to reach out and grab the turquoise sentiment crushed between their unyielding hands. He took a slow, steadying breath before he forged on. "However, I can promise you this much, Josefina. It was not meant to be callous. This ribbon has never been worn by anyone other than you."

Josefina sniffed. "I don't understand. Madame Bonheur told me about how the ribbon belonged to your Colette."

"Fina, you cannot believe a word that woman says. She's little better than the devil himself," Nacho insisted. "And please don't refer to her as *my* Colette."

"But she was. You married her."

"Yes, I married her. However, I did it because I thought she was carrying my child."

Josefina gasped. "You have a child?"

"No," Nacho whispered, his eyes squeezed tightly shut. He shook his head as if trying to mentally clear away whatever image must have plagued him. "Colette went into labor long before the baby was due. They were both lost."

Her grip on his hand tightened. "Ay, pobrecito. I'm so sorry. Losing your mujer had to be difficult enough, but to lose a child? I wouldn't wish that on an enemy."

Suddenly moved, she pulled her hands out of his and crossed him. "Que Dios te bendiga," she said and placed a gentle kiss on his forehead.

Her lips were soft against his skin and he wished she had lingered a little longer, but knew it would have been inappropriate for her to do so while petitioning a blessing on his behalf.

"Thank you," he said as she sat back again. "It's something I've accepted, though. The truth is, it wasn't too hard to move past that time in my life. Rumor had it that even while we were married, Colette had never given up her questionable profession – that she still accepted gentlemen callers whenever I wasn't around. In fact, some even said that it was highly probable the child wasn't even mine. Not that I didn't care about their passing, of course! I'm simply explaining why it was so important for me to find a devout, domesticated wife when I volunteered to marry. I'm so thankful I found you. Will you please give me another chance?"

This time it was he who initiated a kiss – a benevolent one on her hand almost too reverent to describe, but echoing the same earnest plea he had spoken moments before. A part of her rejoiced in the fact that he still wanted to make things work between them – that he would forgive the coldness she had shown him over such a trivial matter as a silly piece of string.

There was another part of her, though, a fragmented piece that maliciously jabbed at her troubled conscience. She was not the divine creature he conceived her to be, but a liar parading around as something she wasn't. She knew the only right thing to do was to be upfront with him about her own troubled past, but the idea of admitting that she was less than what he desired frightened her. She was beginning to like him and the idea of being married to someone like Nacho appealed to her. What if she confessed her own sordid story and decided he wanted to cancel their contract?

She shifted the baby once more. "You don't have to ask me to give you another chance, Nacho. There's nothing to forgive. In fact, I can see how it was wrong to get upset now that you've explained everything. I should have just talked to you about how I felt from the beginning."

"So, it does not bother you that I was married before?"

She shook her head. "We both have things from our pa –"

"Nacho!"

The interruption forced both of them to look up. Nacho quickly stood, his discomfort quite noticeable as he shifted from one foot to the other and tugged at his shirt collar. He nodded at the two women standing before them.

"Um… hello, Jolie… Felice."

Fina had learned earlier in the morning that the woman was yet another one of Madame's "girls." The first, a darker haired woman with a look as sharp as Madame Bonheur's usual expression, cast a brief glance Fina's way. She sniffed a short dismissal and refocused her attention on Nacho. The second women, a petite blonde with s squeaky voice that grated on everyone's nerves, strutted towards him. She wrapped her arms around Nacho's neck.

"Did you miss me, sweetie? I sure missed you."

She raised up on her toes and planted a kiss on Nacho's cheek. The bold action forced Fina out of her seat. She promptly stood, completely forgetting about her sprained ankle. The immediate pain that seared down her foot reminded her and she winced.

Nacho wormed his way out of Felice's grip to embrace Fina. "Are you okay?"

"Yes," she said and shifted the baby to the opposite hip. "My foot is still a little swollen from yesterday."

Jolie spoke up. "We heard about that, dear. Such a... pity."

The expression on the woman's face read anything other than what she professed. A slight smirk tugged at one corner of her mouth, and Fina would have sworn there was a bright glow in her eyes – almost as if the woman delighted to see others in pain.

Or maybe it was the fact that she knew the real cause behind yesterday's accident. Fina had sought out Penny to explain that it wasn't the woman's fault at all. It was that wretched Madame Bonheur. The more Fina thought about it, the more she distinctly recalled feeling something coil around her foot as she danced near that dreadful woman.

That shameful sinner intentionally stuck a foot out to trip her!

However, it was impossible for Fina to inform her friend of the truth since she was nowhere to be found. Surely, the woman was avoiding Fina (and possibly all the others) with the hope that no more of her "bad luck" would rub off on them. Not that Josefina was really worried about such. She had abandoned her former life when she escaped Hank. Now she offered up prayers, burned sage and lit inscribed candles every Sunday in the name of all that was holy, all of which protected her from irrational superstitions.

"Perhaps it's best if I leave," Nacho broke the silence. "I only stopped by to bring you this."

He walked back over to the chair he sat in earlier. For the first time, Fina noticed the book that he had brought with him.

"What's that, sweetie? You bring us a gift?" Felice thrusted her hands out for the book, but Nacho held it away.

"No, I did not." He gave her a stern glare until she finally got the message.

Felice shrugged. "I'm not much for reading anyway. Come on, Jolie. Let's get out of here. We don't need these people or their toffee-nosed morality rubbing off on us."

Fina refrained from stating what was on her mind. She couldn't say much about Jolie, but if what she heard about Felice was even remotely true, then the woman could use a good dose of morality. From her understanding, the woman had abandoned her family – much like Fina's own mother. Leaving behind a husband and two small children, she sought to make a fortune on the stage. However, her aspirations of becoming an actress flopped. So, she turned to whoring in order to support herself. No one knew if it was because she simply didn't want to return home, or if her husband refused to take her back. Either way, she stuck with Madame Bonheur with the plan to one day take over *La Maison*.

When Nacho failed to act remorseful of her declaration to leave, Felice finally turned up her straight, pretty nose. With Jolie by her side, she strutted out the room, stopping only long enough to cast one last look at the Mexican man who vexed her. He still wore a look of disgust – in part over the woman's behavior as well as the fact that he had once been intimately involved with her.

He turned to Josefina, remorse lacing his words. "I find myself once again in the position to ask for your forgiveness. I was young and stupid when I first moved to this town. I didn't realize getting involved with Madame Bonheur could be so damaging."

Josefina stilled. She felt the blood drain from her face, a dizzying rush forcing her to relax further into the chair. She gave baby Jem a comforting squeeze. Then she placed the child down on the blanket beside the chair to play for a few minutes, and tried standing once again, placing all her weight on her good foot. Nacho reached out to steady her, but she waved away his assistance. She looked him squarely in the eyes.

"You were involved with the Madame herself?"

Nacho paled. "Ay que no! That's not what I meant at all. I won't go into details, but let me say that even I'm not that brave. I would *never* touch that woman."

"Just the women who work for her," Josefina pressed.

"No," Nacho insisted. "Not all of them. There was Colette – who you already know I stole away and married. Felice was nothing more than an accident because I missed having Colette around."

"You must have loved her very much then."

Josefina fought to keep the sadness out of her voice, but failed miserably. There was something depressing about fighting against a ghost for a man's heart.

"Honestly? We got on well enough. That is, as well as could be expected. I don't think either one of us was truly in love with the other, though." Nacho focused on the book he still held, picking at a corner of the binding that had started to unravel. He finally left it be and looked back up. "I think it was more a matter of her wanting someone willing to be the father of her unborn child, and my desire to have a family clouding my better judgment. So, I did it. I married her even though some of the other men said I was bien loco – that I shouldn't mess with her because she would never be faithful."

His explanation made it apparent that she wouldn't be measured against another woman should they marry. It gave her hope that she could maybe be good enough for him... if he wouldn't judge her for her own past transgressions.

"Oye, Nacho. You shouldn't be so hard on yourself... or on her." She looked for an opening to reveal her past. "Sometimes people do things out of desperation."

"I know," Nacho said, cutting Fina off. He approached her and handed out the book once more. "However, it's better that the issue doesn't exist to begin with. That's why I'm so thankful that I was one of the men chosen. I'm so grateful that Mrs. Walters found me someone like you – a woman I feel confident to share my family's greatest secrets with."

Josefina swallowed hard, unsure of exactly what she should say. Fear encased her heart, reminding her that it was dangerous to tell him that she had once been little better than the women who worked for Madame Bonheur. The only real difference was that she had been more of a dancing girl. Still, there had been evening visitors – plenty of them – to worm their way in and out of her bedroom.

She looked down at the book in his hands and gently accepted it. "Muchas gracias."

"De nada." He slowly opened his hand to reveal the bunched-up turquoise string. "A woman such as yourself is more worthy than secondhand goods. I will burn this and buy another that is even better."

Josefina's hand quickly wrapped around his. "No, don't do that. It's not really secondhand, if you think about it. Besides, I would be honored to accept any gift you give me."

She pulled the colorful cord from his hand, leaving his free to reach out and stroke her hair.

"You are too good," he said and leaned forward, his lips gently grazing hers.

She tipped her head back, encouraging the kiss to grow deeper. Full of him, both her mouth and body burned with desire. A feeling rushed through her – one that she could only compare to precariously balancing on the brink of a cliff. The fall was inevitable but came with the assurance that she had also been granted wings, and her heart soared when she pulled away to find his eyes full of the same intense yearning she felt.

A squeal from below broke the passionate moment. Heat raced through Fina and she laughed.

"Oh, is that what you think?" She reached down and picked up the precious babe again. "I suppose you're right. Your mother might not approve of you seeing such things at so young an age."

Nacho chuckled. "I hope that's not the case. Once we're married, I plan on stealing kisses whenever I want... and our children will just have to accept that fact."

Her head snapped back up. Their own children? With the life she had lived, she hadn't really given the subject much thought. Now that the idea was planted in her head, she kind of liked it. She bounced baby Jem on her hip. "What do you think of that, nena? Would you like some friends to play with?"

The excitement in Josefina's voice made the baby squeal with delight again, but she liked to think the child was agreeing with her. Children of her own to love would be perfect.

"I think she likes the idea," Nacho said. He lightly grasped Fina's arm and gave it a gentle squeeze. "I must go. The supper rush starts soon. I'll leave the book here for you to look over. Maybe once your ankle heals, you can come down to the diner and we can try making a few of the recipes together."

"I would like that," Fina said.

"Good. Then I'll see myself out."

"Oh, no. Wait a moment and I'll walk you to the door."

"And risk injuring yourself further? I think not, señorita. I can find my way."

"Very well."

With hours of training she managed to perfectly balance on one foot and curtsy. She knew it was an old, outdated custom. Still, she hoped the sentiment wouldn't be lost on him and thrilled to see she was right when he bowed in return, a broad smile painted across his charming face. She waved as he walked away, so elated to think that she would have such a gentleman for a husband that she was almost able to forget all the other troubles that persisted on plaguing her.

CHAPTER 6

*N*oelle, Colorado
December 29, 1876

"YOU STILL HANGING around that pretty little Mexican gal... or does she need a real man to step in and take over?"

The ugly sneer encouraged boisterous laughter from several men who had accompanied Elmer into the diner that morning. It was such a pity, too. The day had begun so well with Nacho's usual morning routine of stepping outside for a bit of fresh air, cold and crisp in his lungs. He walked down to the livery to tend his horses and then back up to begin breakfast for the men who would stumble in, looking for something solid to soak up the rotgut they had drowned themselves in the night before.

Too bad one of those men included the bane of his existence.

"You know what, Elmer? As the owner of this establishment, I would be well within my rights to toss you out anytime I please – same as Seamus."

"You can't do that!"

"Oh, yes, I can… and I most certainly will if you continue making snide remarks about my intended. She is a woman of worth and I will not tolerate another lewd remark like the ones you've been making the past couple of days."

Elmer looked fit to be tied, but there was an audience watching the two men now. He couldn't back down.

"Yeah, well… If she's so sweet on you, then why ain't she down here? Huh? Tell us that."

Nacho sighed with irritation. "As I stated yesterday, she is studying some very special family recipes – *secret* recipes – and they take time to perfect."

"Well how hard can it be to perfect beans? Lord knows that's about all you can cook!"

The jab got Elmer another round of laughs and he hooted with the rest of the men. Nacho prepared to give the oaf a piece of his mind and inform him that he was always more than welcomed to leave if he didn't like the food – and to stay gone for good. But for as quickly as the men had been to poke fun at Nacho, they were just as quick to leave when Sheriff Draven wandered into the diner. Slapping hats on their heads, those who had already paid slipped out the door. The others were quick to throw their money down onto the table – except Elmer. He tossed a few coins onto a dirty plate itself. They sunk into the leftover huevos rancheros, the runny yolks and red sauce thoroughly covering them.

Nacho frowned, but didn't have a chance to speak.

"Mind putting those where they belong?"

The Sheriff glared at Elmer and the man flinched. He immediately fished out the coins, plunked them on the table and then left without another word spoken. Nacho smiled with satisfaction.

"Good day, Draven. A cup of coffee, amigo? No, wait. Perhaps something a little different." Nacho turned to make his way for a cup of chocolate atole, but the sheriff waved away the offer.

"Not today, Nacho. I've got an errand to run." The man waved a stack of papers he carried with him. They looked like sketches.

Nacho quietly wondered if the chore the sheriff had been tasked with might have had anything to do with Pearl. It was no secret the man was attracted to one of Madame Bonheur's ladies. Having been down that path before (and seeing that it led to little more than heartache) Nacho wanted to warn him to be careful. However, Draven was the sort of man who made his own decisions in life. Besides, Pearl seemed different from the women he had known. Perhaps everything would work out in the end.

"Well, if you aren't here to eat, then how can I help you?" Nacho finally asked, picking up a wet cloth to wipe down one of the tables. "I hope there's no kind of trouble. Unless, of course, it has something to do with Elmer Copperpot and you're wanting to make an arrest."

He gave the sheriff a wink and the man laughed.

"Sorry, friend. Nothing like that. I'm just looking for a little information. Thought you might know a thing or two since folks got to eat. Maybe you've heard tale of a few strangers wandering around town? Any gossip about a couple of roughriders roaming around?"

Nacho mulled over the sheriff's question. "You know, come to think of it, I did overhear a couple of men say something last night. It was only in passing, though. I was walking past one of the tables when I specifically heard old man Moses say that he'd never seen a scarier looking bunch – all big and likely to chew leather for dinner."

"Is that so?"

"Asi es."

Draven appeared pensive for a moment. He waved

around the stack of papers again. "Alright. I've got to get these drawings delivered. There might even be one in there for your bride if the two of you ever get around to saying vows."

"Believe me, Sheriff, I'm trying."

Nacho didn't feel like going into further detail and Draven didn't seem to mind that at all. "Well, let me know if you come across any strangers."

"You think there might be some kind of trouble?"

"Nah. Nothing like that. I just like knowing what going on in the town I protect. So, keep me posted. Deal?"

"Claro que si. You'll be the first person I notify."

Draven nodded with satisfaction and made his way back out of the diner. Seeing that most of the work had been completed, Nacho decided to close up as well. There was still plenty of day left and he wanted to spend it with Josefina. He tossed the washcloth on the counter and grabbed his coat off a nearby rack, so eager to leave that he almost forgot to lock the door.

"We wouldn't want another Grandpa Gus incident," he whispered to himself.

The man was harmless and nothing had come to pass the last time, but who knew what could happen given the wrong circumstances. What if the old man got a wild hair to make something to eat and burned himself on the stove? Nacho would feel terrible if the viejo got hurt while in his restaurant.

Nacho climbed up into the wagon, thankful he had thought ahead to prepare it for a ride out of town. He made his way to *La Maison*, pulling up right as Josefina was stepping out.

"Buenas," he greeted her in the familiar afternoon tradition and jumped down from the wagon. She laughed at his boyish charm.

"Good after noon, Nacho." She awarded him with a bright smile as he approached. "Would you like to come in and visit with me?"

"Actually, I was hoping you were coming to visit me." He took hold of her hand and kissed it, all the while drinking in the sight of her. The ribbon was once again woven through her thick braid, which hung over one shoulder. Small, curly ringlets had worked their way loose, though. They framed her cherubic face in a way to make her eyes appear larger and livelier than normal. He breathed in the familiar soft scent of lavender and whispered, "you look ravishing."

She blushed. "You always say the sweetest things. Thank you. Also, my ankle is feeling much better. However, I still don't think I'm in a position to walk all the way to the diner. Otherwise, I would have gladly visited earlier."

"I did not mean for you to walk down to the diner," he said. He gave her hand an extra squeeze and bowed before her. "Would you do me the great honor of visiting my home, señorita?"

Josefina grew excited. "Do you mean the homestead you told me about yesterday?"

"Eso es," he confirmed. The revelation of him owning a home outside of town had come up while they poured over his mother's recipe book the day before. He still wasn't sure which brought him more joy – the fact that she was learning the recipes so well, or the reality that returning to the homestead he had briefly shared with Colette didn't bother him as much. For as easily as his mind had conjured up her name, it swiftly drifted back out. He smiled at the idea of finally moving beyond his past. "So, is that a yes?"

She nodded eagerly. "Of course. I'll go get my coat."

She wandered off and returned a few minutes later, coat donned and carrying a small bag. "I grabbed a few things in case we get hungry."

"With two fine cooks as ourselves? It would never happen!"

When she didn't laugh at his joke, he helped her up into the wagon and climbed in after her.

"Is it far?" she asked.

He took hold of the reins and gently snapped them. "Not too much. It's just on the outskirts of town – a couple of miles from Zeke Kinnison."

"Ah, yes. I know who he is. I think one of the women are interested in him – or maybe it is reverse. I could not say. Nonetheless, it would be kind of nice to have neighbors… while still not being *too* terribly close."

"Yes, that is why I chose the nice little spot I have. That way there is solitude, but not so much to be completely secluded. Also, it would allow me to be far enough away from any rowdy dealings in town but still close enough to get to the diner quickly."

Josefina frowned. "You said 'rowdy dealings.' I suppose I should have asked this before, but is Noelle a dangerous place?"

"No, not really. Some of the guys can get a little rough sometimes, but it's nothing different than what you would find in any other town. Really, the folks here in Noelle are a good bunch." An image of Elmer Copperpot purposely throwing his money into his plate of food appeared. He added, "Well, except maybe one or two guys. They aren't anything to worry about, though. More annoying than dangerous."

A comfortable silence settled between them as they rode out of town and down the long, winding road some ways. Fina became animated again.

"Nacho, look!" She pointed to a family of deer jetting through a field they passed. "I haven't seen any of them in a while. They aren't that common in Denver. At least, not inside of town."

"Fortunately, you'll see plenty of them out this way. I remember I once thought I heard one of the horses neighing. When I opened the front door, it was a beautiful buck. I guess he was talking to his lady friend, telling her it was okay to come out to play for a while."

Josefina clapped her hands. "How exciting! I can't wait to see your home."

"Well, you won't have to wait long. It's just over this crest."

They rounded the top of the hill and a quaint, snow covered cabin surrounded by barren trees and a frozen pond came into view.

"Ay, Nacho, it's gorgeous. If my ankle was completely healed, I would jump down and run to it!"

Nacho laughed, pleased to see she was taken with the place. "When I first arrived in town, I had the same plan as everyone else. I wanted to strike gold. However, I also wanted to live in a place where I could safely hide it – instead of doing so in a little tent out in the bush, or a rented room in one of the saloons. Both are easy ways to lose your money through drink or theft. So, I bought the land with the money from my part of the ranch I inherited. Then I set to work on the homestead."

The wagon drew up to the house and Nacho grimaced. After Colette had passed, he had really let the place go. With a yard full of dead trees half covered in snow, the crusted windows further declared the terrible neglect the place had suffered.

"I know it isn't much to look at right now, but it has a lot of potential. All it needs is a woman's touch."

Josefina grew serious as Nacho climbed down and offered her a hand. "Didn't it already have one?"

"If you speak of Colette, then not really." He offered his

arm and when she accepted, folded her hand into the crook of it. They made their way to the front porch. "She only stayed here the last couple of months of her pregnancy. In the beginning, she preferred to stay in town at the diner."

"Is that where the French-looking dressing screen came from? The one in the room attached to the diner's kitchen?"

Nacho nodded. "I guess staying in town gave her a better opportunity to continue making money by entertaining other…"

He trailed off and looked away. Fina's grip on his arm tightened.

"I hope you know I would never do anything like that."

Her words would have put him at ease, but the look in her eyes was fearful. Had he said something to indicate she would?

"The thought didn't even cross my mind, but enough talk about that. I don't want to bring the past into our present anymore."

She nodded in agreement. "Yes, let's see the inside of your home."

He wanted to correct her and say "*our* home," but refrained. Despite her seeming strength of character, there were moments when she reminded him of the deer they had just seen in the field. Beautiful and strong, yet easily frightened if approached wrong. Besides, it wouldn't really be their home until they married. That is, if they ever got around to saying "Si, acepto." They had both made references to how things would be *after* the fact, but kept dancing around the discussion of accomplishing the deed itself. Worse, he didn't know how or when to broach the subject. The first time around had been easy. The woman was pregnant. He stepped up to take care of "his" responsibility. However, there were no clear instructions this time around. Add to that the fact that he had never felt this connected to someone before…

"Ignacio, are you feeling well?"

Nacho looked down at Josefina and realized he had mentally wandered off.

"Forgive me. I was lost in thought. I honestly can't recall the way this place looks," he lied.

"Do you wish me to wait out here while you go... straighten up?"

He gathered she must have thought he was worried she would find more of Colette's things laying around – like the dressing screen in the diner's single room apartment. He had given those things away, though. Clothes, shoes, and various little trinkets had made their way back to the other ladies at *La Maison,* all of whom had been only too happy to snatch them up – like birds pecking over the leftover crumbs he shook from the bread tray each morning.

"No," he finally said. "There's no need for you to keep standing out in the cold. Just be forewarned that it might not be as tidy as the restaurant."

He opened the door and invited her in. Before them was everything as he had remembered. The front room had two sitting chairs with a small table between them and a fireplace. Off to the right was the dining room with the kitchen on the other side of that. To the left of the parlor was a staircase that wrapped itself up to where two bedrooms awaited.

"I see what you mean," she said and ran a gloved hand over a nearby table covered in dust. Her fingers made deep grooves, revealing that the table still had a deep cherry color to it beneath all the muck. Dust floated into the air, tickling their noses forcing them both to cough.

"Like I said, it's been a while since I've visited the place. Perhaps it would be better if you waited outside until I get it all cleaned up."

"Nonsense," she replied. "I'll be cleaning it regularly once we're married. No harm in beginning the chore a little early."

"Yes, about that…"

"Hmm?"

He tugged at his collar and cleared his throat again. "Yes, you were quite right in your assessment. Perhaps it would be best if we helped clean the place together. I'll just start a fire first and try to get the place a little warmed up."

He went about getting the kindling lit and added a few logs that had remained by the fireplace from long ago. Soon, a small blaze crackled in the stone hearth and he went off in search of rags and a large bucket. He returned a few minutes later.

"We have a well but I figure it's probably frozen," he explained and showed her the bucket full of snow. "Besides, more work to draw up water when the snow will melt soon enough."

"Let's set it by the fire and it will melt even quicker," Josefina suggested. The long, thin branches of a nearby tree caught her attention as they whipped back and forth in the breeze, their gnarled fingers scratching at the window. "In the meantime, I can go for the recipe book. I left it out in the wagon."

Nacho looked up as well. "Perhaps that's a good idea."

Josefina donned her coat again. She barely had cracked the door open when the knob tore free from her hand, the door flying open. She cried out in dismay. "Oh, no!"

Nacho felt the way Josefina looked – completely horrified to see pages of his mother's recipe book sucked out from between the leather binding only to fly through the air before landing in the patches of wet snow. The precious papers tumbled along the yard, racing towards the frozen pond.

He sprinted down the stairs. "Quick! We can still catch them if we hurry."

Fina followed, frantic at the thought that she would be to

blame if she couldn't return the book as new. She made a mad dash for a paper that floated over a stump and then landed close by. She snatched up the recipe and, filled with triumphant glee, waved it in the air.

"I've got one," she declared as she turned to find Nacho and saw him carefully stepping onto the pond. She yelled, "What are you doing?"

"I've got them all except that one right there," Nacho said.

She looked to where he pointed, chagrined to see that a single sheet had come to quietly rest in the middle of the pond. Ignoring the slight pain in her foot, she rushed towards the pond as quickly as she could. "Párate, Ignacio! Don't go out there. You'll fall through."

Nacho stiffened at the sound of the suggestion. "Then what do you suggest we do? The wind has died down and it might get stuck out there for who knows how long. Besides, the pond is frozen."

He stomped his foot to prove his point. He turned back to her. "See?"

Thankful she had worn sensible shoes, she slipped out onto the ice with him and saw that he was right. It was indeed frozen. She slid a little, her arms waving wildly. She filled with embarrassment at the fact that she could twirl on her toes for minutes at a time, but could hardly keep her balance on the glass pool.

"Like this," Nacho said. He grabbed hold of her hands and helped her center. Once she found her balance, he pulled her a little towards him. They spun around together, laughing. "Hey, you're pretty good at this!"

"I better be," Josefina laughed. "I'm the best dancer at…"

She inhaled sharply, surprised that she had almost revealed that she had been a dancer at Hank's Whisky River Saloon. Nacho's eyes narrowed. "You're the best *what*?"

She pulled away and ran her hands down the front of her

dress, busying herself with smoothing it out. "I meant to say I *was* the best dancer at home – back when I still lived with my parents and my sister, Elena."

His eyes were filled with uncertainty, but his smile offered nothing but understanding. "Well, then you'll surely have the town at a disadvantage should there ever be a fiesta. I've seen you move, and if you are anything at all as your name would imply, then I believe you would dance circles around us all."

She smiled uncomfortably. While she appreciated the compliment, it only served as a further reminder of her old life. Unlike her family who had called her Fina as a shortened form of her full name, men in the saloon used it as a translation to mean she was as "fine" in bed as she was on stage.

The wind began to pick up again.

"Ay, caray! I better get the recipe," Nacho said.

"I'll go get it," she offered and started out towards the middle of the pond. She slowly slid her feet along the ice, looking down at the glossy mirror that shined back at her. She reached the page and bent forward to retrieve it, noticing the strange color beneath when she lifted it up. She called back to Nacho, pointing. "Isn't that interesting? The ice is darker here... and, look. It's almost black over there."

His face went ashen.

"Fina, get off the pond." Nacho backed away, fearful that any additional weight would force the ice to cave in. He reached the bank and called out again. "Hurry!"

"Why?" she asked as she stepped forward.

A cracking sound made her look back down and she finally realized then that the ice had appeared darker because it was thinner; the dark spot was water that hadn't yet frozen.

Another pop of the ice fracturing below her feet spurred

her into action. Firmly clutching the paper to her chest, she skated forward as quickly as she dared.

"That's it," Nacho encouraged. He reached out to grab hold of her. "You're almost there."

Another sound of the ice popping – this time all around her – made her freeze. "I don't think I can make it."

Nacho looked around the yard behind him and took off running.

"Where are you going?" Fina cried out, fear welling up inside her.

He grabbed a thick branch that had fallen off a dying tree and made his way back to her. He carefully held it out over the pond. "For this. Now grab hold."

Fina crumpled up the recipe into a tiny ball and threw it at him. "*Ten.* Catch!"

He did as instructed, bending forward to snatch the paper up from where it landed beside his feet. In so doing, the branch dipped, smacking hard against the ice, producing a glorious cracking noise. Nacho shot back up. He tightened his grip on the bough just as the frozen crystal gave way to a monstrous vision of Josefina slipping into cold, wet jaws beneath her.

"Josefina!"

She bobbed back up to the surface with a scream, furiously splashing about. Nacho dropped the branch to the ground, along with the recipe so he could better grip the thick limb as he laid his body on top of it, anchoring it to the bank. "Grab hold!"

Eyes wide with terror and heart full of fright, she latched onto the tiny bit of salvation before her, clinging to the branch for dear life.

"I need you to try to pull yourself towards me. Can you do that?"

The frosty winter air bit into her bones, but she nodded

all the same and did as she was told. One hand worked itself in front of the other as she got on with the tedious task, slowly hefting herself closer towards the bank and Nacho. Her arms shook from the sheer strength required to pull her weight, magnified by a multiple she couldn't possibly fathom from all the water that must have gathered in the heavy dress she bore. When she was finally within arm's length, they reached out for one another.

Josefina let out a wretched sob as Nacho pulled her onto the embankment and held her close.

"Ya, ya. No llores, chiquitita."

He could have sat there, continuing to comfort her, but the chattering of teeth beside his ear served as a reminder that she was soaked straight through. He stood, pulling her up with him. "Come. We must get you inside by the fire before you get sick."

She allowed him to lead her back to the house, the chilly wind nipping at her, numbing the tip of her nose along with her ears, fingers and toes. By the time she reached the door and stumbled into the sitting room, she wondered if there was a single part of her with any feeling left at all.

"Stand here by the fire and I will help you get out of those wet clothes."

She raised a brow at the suggestion. "And here I thought you were a gentleman."

"I am," he said and then realized she was teasing him. A smile lit his face. "I won't look… too much."

She laughed and allowed him to remove her coat. Then he began unbuttoning the back of her top dress, his fingers deftly moving down her back. With only the thin cotton shift left, he left her to sit beside the fire as he ran upstairs to fetch a dry set of clothes and blankets. When he returned she had already removed her boots and had peeled off one of her wet stockings.

"I'm afraid I don't have anything for your feet," he explained and handed them to her. He turned around to offer her some small form of privacy as she slipped out of the wet undergarments and into the clothes he offered. "Nor do I have any women's dresses left. So, you'll have to make due with some of my attire."

The idea of donning his dead wife's wardrobe didn't appeal much to Josefina. So, she was fine with the fact that there was only one of his oversized button-up shirts and long johns to wear. However, cold feet were far less desirable than she wished to admit.

"Thank you for the clothes," she said. "You can turn back around now."

He did so and the sight of his shirt hanging loose off her slender body ignited a small, desirous blaze within. Clearing his throat to remind himself that now was not the moment to feel amorous, he stepped forward and wrapped the blanket around her, his hand lightly brushing against the nape of her neck. Her cold skin stung his own flesh, effectively cooling him. He directed her back towards the fire. "You're still too cold. Sit here and warm up while I make you some *té de manzanilla*."

"You have chamomile? I thought you said you didn't stay out here anymore."

"I don't," he explained. "However, I still try to keep some of the basics. Just wait here while I prepare it."

He picked up the bucket of snow they had filled earlier and carried it to the kitchen.

"I suppose it's good we didn't use it to clean the house with," she called out to him as he found a pot and lit the small wood burning stove. It warmed quicker than she had anticipated. With a fire roaring beside her and a warm glow behind her back, Josefina could feel life crawl back through her body. She snuggled down deep into the blanket and enjoyed the warmth that filled the dusty little cabin. A tiny sneeze escaped.

"That is exactly what I feared," Nacho said as he returned to her side. He held out a mug with dried flowers still floating around in it, the withered buds staining the water with a soft yellow tinge. "You're catching a cold."

She accepted the hot tea. "I think it's more the fact that the house is still dusty."

Nacho turned to retrieve his coat. "I'll go fetch some more snow and get to cleaning it."

"No, don't do that." She patted the floor beside her. "Sit with me for a while. There is something I wanted to give you."

He did as requested and she reached into the blanket with her free hand, pulling up a fist on the return. "I think you dropped this."

She opened her hand to reveal a ball of crumpled paper. Nacho's eyes grew wide with surprise.

"I can't believe you saved it," he said and graciously accepted the recipe.

"I hated the idea of losing something so precious," she explained. "It is hard enough to lose a parent. I wouldn't want you to lose your legacy, too."

"*Ay, mi Fina.*" He leaned forward and gently ran the back of his hand down her face. "You don't know how much this means to me. Between this page and the ones I stuck in my coat pocket, we still have almost all the recipes. At the very least, we have enough to create some incredible dishes at the restaurant. What can I do to thank you?"

"What can you do to thank *me?* Nacho, you just saved my life."

He clucked his tongue. "That is nothing. Anyone would have done that. Come, there must be something you wish for."

She bit the inside of her cheek. What she wanted more than anything was to be reunited with her father and sister. Although, was that really true? She considered the last few days with Nacho. They had been comfortable ones filled with revealing moments and the small, surprising revelation that she liked the idea of marriage to him – for no other reason than to be with him. Of course, she wanted to find what was left of her family and try to put the pieces back together again. However, she didn't want to do so at Nacho's expense. Asking such a favor was too much.

"Well?" he pressed her.

She stretched her feet in front of her, shaking them. "Are you sure you don't have any socks? My feet are still freezing."

"I can honestly say I unfortunately do not have anything for your feet."

She frowned and nodded to where her leggings hung beside the fireplace. "Then I guess the best I can wish for is that my stockings dry out quickly."

"Not so fast," Nacho said and reached out for her feet. "Oooh, you weren't kidding. You have chilly toes."

She giggled. "What are you doing?"

"What does it look like? I'm going to help warm them up. Now drink your tea. It will make you strong."

"I know," she said as he began to massage the tops of her feet. "My grandmother was a *curandera*."

Surprise lit Nacho's face as he gently worked around her ankles. "Was she really?"

"Mmm, asi es."

"Oh, does that mean you're going to read my fortune? Eh? Maybe tell me what are in those tea leaves."

"Don't be silly. I said she was a healer – not a fortune teller," she admonished him. A coy smile tugged at a corner of her mouth. "Besides, it was my cup of tea – not yours."

He baited her. "Then tell me… what is in your future?"

She looked down at the near empty cup and squinted. A mischievous look filled her eyes and she scrunched her nose, pretending to read the leaves. "It says I'm going to marry soon."

His hands stilled for a moment as he studied her dark eyes. They were filled with humor. He shrugged and looked back down.

"That might very well be true," he said and began massaging her feet again. He pinched one of her toes. "I think I could get used to looking at these little *salchichas*."

"Nacho!" Josefina squealed and tried to pull her feet back. He held on to them, though. "How dare you make fun of my feet. They do not look like sausages."

He roared with laughter and held on even tighter to her feet, trying to pull her closer. When she wouldn't budge, he scooted forward. "Oh, don't be mad, amor. I couldn't help myself."

She turned her pretty nose up, feigning indignation. "You made fun of me."

"Never," he said. "I think your feet are beautiful. I love them and everything else about you, too."

She turned back to find his face full of sincerity and for one brief moment she was full of hope. But then she remembered the lie she was still living. She sighed. "Ay, Nacho. You say that now, but we hardly know one another. What if you find out something about me that you don't like?"

"Cómo que, Fina? What do you think you could possibly say to make me change my mind?" He waited expectantly for an answer. When she failed to give even one, he made his own list of attributes he appreciated, ticking one after the other off his fingers. "Fina, I love how you are kind, but not too soft or weak. You are made of strong stuff. That's obvious just by looking at you. Oh, and to speak of looks. Well, let's just say you are no ugly duckling. *Acuerdo?* That's a good thing. You know? Because I've looked in the mirror once or twice and I don't think I'm so bad either."

He wagged his brows at her and she snickered. "*Ay, tan chistoso.* And here I thought you were trying to convince me of all *my* great qualities – not yours."

"I was talking about you. I just thought I might throw one in for me, too. Maybe that would help you decide I'm the right choice."

"Nacho, why would you think otherwise?"

"Well, you know, some of the other men have already exchanged their vows. I figured maybe we hadn't because you weren't too sure about how you felt about me."

She stared at him, astonished. Could he really think the reason they hadn't made it to the alter was because of *her*? If she thought about it long enough, she supposed she had seemed somewhat inaccessible. Every time he would come over to *La Maison,* she had been too busy helping the other women to return with him to the diner. If she wasn't watching the baby for Zee, then she was trying to convince Penny that she didn't really have bad luck. Then there was Minnie who she had tried to reach out to, but the woman appeared to be hiding even more than Josefina herself. Every conversation with the woman would dead end into thick air.

So, Josefina had done what little she could do – studied the recipe book Nacho lent her and practiced a dish or two, hoping to impress him when he came for his daily visit between the breakfast and dinner rush.

The dinner rush!

"Nacho, what time is it? Shouldn't you be back at the diner?"

Nacho's head whipped around. He looked at the dark-ening sky and jumped up. "*Ay, caray*! I completely lost track of time. You're right. I'll have to get back quickly… but your clothes. They are not dry yet."

She stood and joined him beside the hanging wet clothes. She grabbed hold of the fabric and squeezed. Large drops of water splashed to the floor beneath. "You're right. They're still far too damp to put back on… and I most certainly can't go back into town wearing your shirt and a blanket."

"Ha! Most definitely not."

"Then I guess there is no other choice but for me to stay here tonight."

"I don't know," Nacho hesitated. "The idea of you out here all alone by yourself… I suppose it would be fine for a short while. There is still a rifle upstairs in one of the bedrooms – not that I think you would need it of course. Still, it is there in case some animal was to come looking for trouble."

"Then I guess it's a good thing I know how to shoot." She patted his arm. "*No te preocupes, Nacho.* I'll be fine."

He nodded his agreement. "Very well. I will go out to the restaurant and get dinner served and return as soon as the last customer leaves. *Sale?*"

"Yes, that sounds like a lovely idea." She lifted up onto the tips of her toes and leaned in, lightly brushing her lips against his cheek. "Be safe, *amorcito.*"

He stood, staring at her as if he had forgotten how to say goodbye. Finally, he reached for his coat and slid it on, followed by his hat. He touched the brim of it and quietly slipped out the door.

CHAPTER 7

*J*osefina dipped the rag into the water once again and scrubbed the step before her. It was the top rung of the dusty staircase and she couldn't wait to get it clean so she could check out the bedrooms. She supposed she could have done that sooner, but now that she had rid the downstairs of all its filth, she refused to track a bunch of dirt and dust through the newly cleaned house upon descending. Speaking of clean…

She looked down at the water and grimaced. The murky water had turned dark – it's terrible color reminding her of the thin pond ice. She shuddered, knowing it was more from the thought of the ordeal than any actual cold. Despite the fire dying down to little more than glowing embers, the house still remained wonderfully warm and inviting. She hated the idea of going back outside to dump the water and retrieve more fresh snow, but the idea of having the entire house cleaned before Nacho returned delighted her.

"Oh, well. Let's go, feet."

Thankful that her stockings and boots had dried, she bounced down the stairs, silently laughing at how she must look with the long johns and shirt to match. *Perhaps I'll start a new fashion.* The thought made her laugh until she remembered that her clothes were still wet. That meant she would have to venture out with the blanket wrapped around her again. She could only be thankful there would be no one to witness the display.

Clutching the rope handle, she passed the table and picked up the lantern she had left there. Thank goodness she had found it while cleaning the living room earlier. Night had descended rather quickly and despite all the stars in the sky, she liked the idea of having a little extra light to see by – especially on such a cold, spooky night. The tree branches looked like long fingers reaching out to snatch her up, and the wind whispered terrifying stories.

Stepping off the porch, she carefully placed the lantern down and walked several feet away before tossing the dirty water. It sunk into the snow, scarring the perfect white fluff with a dark jagged scar. She turned away and walked a little further in the opposite direction and then knelt down the best she could with the blanket wrapped around her. She scooped a few handfuls of snow into the bucket and then stopped to wipe her hand her hand along the blanket, rubbing until there was feeling in it once again. With her hand warmed, she repeated the procedure of gathering more snow. Once the bucket was full and her hand felt somewhat normal, she stood and walked back towards the lantern, picking it up as she made her way to the house, pausing only momentarily as she studied the tracks in the snow.

I never realized how big Nacho's feet are, she thought as she placed her own foot beside a larger print heading in the same direction as hers, back towards the front steps. She made her way up them, again stopping.

She had purposely left the door wide open for a little light to illuminate the porch, but now her mind played tricks on her, casting shadows where she knew they could not be.

"*No seas sonsa,*" she chided herself. "You're the only one here, silly."

In a show of false bravado, she puffed up her chest – not that it was all noticeable beneath the blanket. However, it did give her a small measure of courage. Gripping the bucket and blanket in one hand, and the lamp in the other, she entered the house and slammed the door.

"You might as well come out right now," she demanded and raised the lantern high above her head. "I have no problem setting this place ablaze with both of us in it."

Only the crackling of the fire in the stone hearth answered her. She shook her head, mumbling. "I'm losing my mind."

Walking towards the fireplace, she set the lamp on the mantle and stoked the embers, deciding to add another log since the fire in the wood burning stove had already died out. She looked around, deciding that the fireplace would provide enough light and the lantern would provide what she needed upstairs.

The wood on the second step creaked as she made her way towards the bedrooms, as did the landing once she reached the top. Choosing the room closest to her, she veered left and smiled at the fact that much of the room was bathed in moonlight. She set the lamp down and examined the few belongings that were there – a bed, dresser and wash stand with bowl and pitcher. She quickly lost interest in them and turned to leave when a white gleam caught the corner of her eye. It was a white cotton sheet draped over something large and rectangular. She walked over and slowly pulled the cover off. Awestruck by its revelation, she dropped the fabric to the ground and reverently ran her hand over a large painting with a gold frame. A young, thick braided woman wearing traditional Mexican garb heading out of the market place, smiling at the bounty she carried in her arms.

Josefina tapped the frame with her nails, the metal clinking under her touch. She pulled it, revealing yet another painting behind it and another after that. Happy families, Aztecan gods, la Virgen de Guadalupe. They all went about their usual endeavors, unaware or uncaring of being observed by the outside world. There was even a painting of a beautiful hacienda – the workers in the field reminding her very much of her grandmother's village so many years ago.

She looked around the room – a hidden treasure trove of cultural gems.

"These should not be concealed in this dark, dusty room," she complained to no one in particular and had scarcely decided that she would drag them out when she heard a noise from downstairs.

She leaned out into the hallway, the lamp raised above her head. "Is that you, Nacho?"

The sound of something scratching made her heart race.

It's probably just the trees again, banging against the windows.

The clash of something metal sent her scurrying back into the room. She looked around in search of anything that could be used to fight off an intruder when she remembered Nacho's mention of the rifle being upstairs "in one of the bedrooms."

It was obviously not in *this* room, though. This one seemed like little more than storage. *So, it must be the other room*, she reasoned and made her way back to the door and peered around the threshold. Satisfied that no one had discovered her, she quietly tiptoed across the hall and into a room that made the bold declaration that a man had claimed the space. Discounting the heaps of clothes laying around the room and a smell that declared they were not the freshest to be found, she spotted the rifle hanging on a wall beside the bed. She yanked it from its resting place when a scuffling sound startled her. She screamed and whirled around, ready to pull the trigger on...

A raccoon!

The creature carried in its hand a shiny coin.

"Hey! Where did you find that?" She bent over to take it from him and he bared his teeth, hissing. She snatched her hand back, the fear of a rabid raccoon scaring her more than the idea of him making off with his plunder. Still, she was angry the little beast had given her such a fright. Refusing to kill it for what came natural, she stomped her foot and swatted at it with one end of the rifle. "Go on, you'll not get anymore. Scat!"

She pushed the raccoon, growling and hissing as loud as she could. It raced out, back down the stairs and into the living room. Josefina circled around it, making her way to the door and opening it wide once she got there. "Go on or I really will shoot."

She swatted at the raccoon yet again, finally coercing the thieving brute out the door. It ran along the porch, not in any great hurry to go anywhere. So, she lifted the rifle and aimed for the sky, the weapon making a terrific noise that scared both she and the raccoon. It jumped off the porch and raced away into the night.

"That's what you get," she yelled after it, throwing out empty threats. "Try to steal our gold again and you'll make a fine stew! My husband can do it. He's a cook!"

With the word "husband" still echoing in her ears, she straightened back up, the revelation surprising her that she had fully accepted their relationship... and for no other reason than the fact that she actually cared for Nacho. The thought sent a delicious shiver down her spine and she shut the door once again, resolute to complete her previous chore and have tidied the entire house before Ignacio returned.

~

NACHO LOOKED up at the house, a warm glow casting a welcoming invitation. This was what he envisioned for himself when he thought about married life – a cozy home filled with cheer and laughter...

And good food, of course.

He thought about the bundle he carried in his arms, sure that the new recipe he tried would delight his Fina.

His Fina.

It hadn't been the first time he thought about it, and he liked it a little more every time the idea ran across his mind. Her slip into the pond had scared the wits right out of him. In fact, he was surprised that he had even remembered to stay calm and take quick action. It also made him very aware of the fact that there were no guarantees in life. In part, he supposed he had hesitated asking her outright to marry him as soon as they met because he wanted to win her affections... but also because the thought of marrying again unnerved him a little bit. No doubt, he wanted to do it. He just wanted to make sure that he wouldn't make a repeat mistake.

Josefina is no Colette.

He nodded firmly. He would not keep dragging his feet on the matter. He was going to walk in and ask her right now, before anything else. He opened the door and confidently strode into the living room... and took in the splendor of all the work she had done.

"Nacho? Is that you?" she called.

He ambled over to the stairs and called up. "Si, it is I. I've returned as I promised with a meal to share, but now I wonder if it's enough."

Fina walked down the stairs, her face smudged with dirt. "Thank goodness. I'm starving."

"It's no wonder. Look at this place," he said with astonishment. "I can't believe you did all of this while I was away."

"Do you like the paintings?" she asked, pointing up to one of the living room walls. "I thought that one looked nice there."

Nacho studied *La Virgen* who in return smiled down on him.

"Yes, I always thought she belonged there, but Col—" his voice trailed off and he handed her the bundle of food he carried. "This is for you."

"Thank you." Josefina eagerly accepted it and sat in one of the chairs not far from the fireplace. "Nacho, I don't want you to feel like you can never mention your past around me. We've talked about this before."

He took the seat across from her. "I know, but I don't really want to bring the past into the future."

"I wish you would reconsider," she said and unwrapped the bundle to reveal a tin plate filled with carnitas and tortillas. "I have so many questions."

"You have questions about my previous marriage?"

"Ah… not so much. What I was wondering about were the paintings you have up in your room. They are beautiful!"

"Gracias. They belonged to my father."

"See, that I would not have guessed. From the little you told me previously, I thought he was a very hard man. So, I would have guessed that it was your mother who had a hand in it all."

"Well, she certainly shared her opinion about what she did and did not want hanging on her walls. However, all these paintings are ones that he had created – some of them even before he knew her." Nacho looked up and pointed to the Virgen of Guadalupe. "Take this one for instance. He painted it for his own mother before he ever even married."

"He actually painted them himself?" she asked, awestruck.

"Some of them. Others were commissioned or purchased outright."

"Then maybe you got your creativity from him," Fina reasoned. "He took to art like you take to cooking."

"I'm not so sure about that," Nacho explained. "I think I may have gotten his determination, though. My father put away his paints once the ranch started growing. He always said that providing for a family required hard work and discipline. So, I try to apply that to what I do now and work as hard as I can at every meal I cook."

"You certainly worked your magic this time," Josefina said. "The food is incredible."

"Not nearly as incredible as this place looks," Nacho again complimented her. It's wonderful to see everything went so well while I was gone."

"Yes, I made sure of it – even if the strangest thing happened tonight."

"What?" He asked, a look of concern crossing his face. "*Qué cosa rara*? Did you see any strangers?"

"Strangers? Why would I? You yourself said there was hardly anyone out this way – except that trapper for a neighbor and even that's several miles away. I said the strangest *thing* happened."

Nacho sighed. "Oh, okay. I guess I got a little nervous when you used that word "strange. Made me think about a conversation I had in town."

Josefina stopped eating, her fork hovering in midair. "Why? What's going on?"

"I'm sure it's nothing. Just some talk in town about these three men a few of the folks have seen. Thing is no one actually knows who they are or where they're staying. So, it's a little concerning – especially for someone like the sheriff." A smiled crossed Nacho's face. "Speaking of which... Did you know that he and Pearl were together?"

Josefina smiled. "I had a feeling they were keen on each other, but I didn't know anything would actually come of it. Do you think they'll get married one day?"

"One day?" Nacho let out a laugh. "I think that time's already come and gone. I was just leaving the diner when I heard they had exchanged vows."

"Really? That's wonderful!"

"It is, but things are still moving too slowly. At this rate, the railroad might still decide to pass us by."

"Yes, I've heard about that being the main reason the men in this town wanted to marry."

"No," Nacho insisted. "That isn't true at all. Many of the men wanted to get married, but who could they possibly choose? It's not like there is much choice in town. The Reverend's plan was a sound one that served more than one purpose – and benefits everyone involved."

She considered his words for a moment and agreed. The women had as much to gain out of the marriages as did the men and the town in general – especially if the rumors were true that the gold had dried up.

Gold!

"Ignacio, I didn't get to tell you what happened."

Nacho threw another log onto the fire and stocked the embers below. "Oh, yes. My apologies for interrupting. What was this strange thing you saw?"

"A raccoon."

Nacho laughed. "*Ay, nena.* That is not so strange."

"Carrying a coin."

"What do you mean he was carrying a coin?"

"Well, you see, I was in the bedroom with all the paintings... Really, those paintings shouldn't be wasting away in a dark corner of a dusty house. They should be hanging in the diner. Wouldn't that be a grand idea?"

"Yes, yes. We can do that. But what were you saying about the raccoon?"

"So, there was this noise. *Ay, me dio miedo.* I was literally shaking in my stockings. So, I grab the gun and I turn around and there he is – this nasty little animal, clutching the coin and hissing at me when I tried to take it from him."

"You should not have tried to take it. He could have been rabid. What if he bit you?"

"That's exactly what I thought," she explained. "So, I shooed him away by pushing him with the butt of the rifle and stomping my feet. I even growled and hissed just like him."

Nacho snorted. "Must have been some fright – seeing a grown woman turn into an animal."

She squinted at him. "Señor, are you making fun of me again?"

"Again?" He feigned confusion. "What are you talking about? I have never made fun of you."

"No? What about my sausage toes from earlier this evening... and let's not forget my 'backwards name.'"

He chuckled and reached out to lightly tug on her braid. "Perhaps I was teasing you a little. Perhaps you deserved it, though."

Josefina stopped chewing. "*Cómo?*"

Nacho leaned forward again and picked at the pulled pork and gave her a nonchalant shrug. "You never did explain why your family name was turned around."

She swallowed hard, the food feeling as if it had stopped somewhere in the middle of her chest. Her shoulders deflated along with her voice. "Oh, that. I suppose it is rather unheard of. You see, my mother left my father when my sister and I were very young. He was angry, of course. So, he decided to follow the same American practice of placing the paternal surname last. This was good for when we went out. Before, the name was so long and people would say 'the Morales children.' Afterwards, we were known as 'the Zapatero girls.'"

A moment of silence passed between them before Nacho finally spoke. "Your mother left your father?"

She had hoped he wouldn't think much about that part – especially since she had swiftly brushed over the fact. "Yes, she did."

"And she left you and your sister behind?"

"For a short time," Josefina explained. "She came back a few years later and reclaimed me."

"But not your sister?"

Eyes brimming with tears, Josefina busied herself with her food, carefully lining a tortilla with meat. She tried speaking, but the words caught in her throat. So, she only shook her head in response.

"That must have been very difficult. How old were you?"

She roughly swiped at her eyes and then looked up. "Eight when she left and fourteen when she returned." She shrugged as if the facts didn't at all bother her and took a bite of food.

Nacho looked at her strangely. "I understand you were very young when this all happened, but I don't understand why you never went back. Didn't you ever think to find your father and sister?"

"Of course, I did! Once I was old enough to be out on my own, I did just that. I went back to our hometown – straight up to our little house – and found it empty. I was frantic, roaming up and down the streets until I found a neighbor who told me that they had left – moved to someplace that even she didn't know... and she knew everything about everyone, because she was *bien chismosa*. That's when I returned to Colorado. I mean, if the town gossip couldn't even give me information, then what else could I do? I could not just sit there and starve. I had to eat, so I had to work. Then I heard about the mail order brides and... *aqui estoy.*"

She waved her arms around her and the plate nearly slid from her lap. She caught it quickly and placed it on the table before looking back up. The strange look on her face made her worry that she had revealed too much. She cleared her throat. "Trust me. If I had been in a position to do everything – take care of myself *and* look for my family – then I would have."

He thought about what she said for a minute. "Is that what you're trying to do now?"

The question made her blood run cold in her veins. "What?"

He leaned forward and stared directly into her face. "You said that if you had been in the right position to do everything, then you would have. Is that why you wanted to get married?"

Her heart gave a solid thud in her chest. She wasn't the fainting sort, but the firm look in his eyes made her feel just that. She could see it now. This was not a man to be lied to. At the same time, she knew she couldn't tell him everything about her sordid past – not *every* little detail.

"Yes," she whispered.

"And now that you have come to know me... would you have married me even if it meant *not* finding your family?"

She nodded fervently, her answer strong. "Yes."

He sat back and looked away, slowly rocking back in his chair as he stared into the fire. He sat that way for so long that she started to wonder if he was ever going to speak to her again. She began to stand and gather the plate of food when he finally said, "Then I will help you find your family."

She went ramrod straight. "What did you say?"

"As my wedding gift to you, I will help find your family."

A bright smile came over her face. "Ignacio, are you asking me to marry you?"

A sheepish grin stretched across his face. "If your answer is 'yes,' then I guess I am."

She dropped the plate back onto the table and rushed forward, wrapping her arms around him. The chair tipped back and he quickly sat forward.

"*Mujer*," He joked, "you're going to kill me like the raccoon."

"Hey!" she poked him hard. "I didn't kill that horrible little thief."

He laughed again. "Now he is a thief, too?"

She groaned. "Just like a man to never listen. I told you that before. He stole the coin. Remember? It was a gold one."

A strange look came over his face. "A gold coin?"

"Yes, that's what I said. Although I don't know where in the world he could have found it. I cleaned this whole place. There's no gold anywhere in it."

"No," he said, a strange look reflecting in his eyes. "You are right about that. There's no gold in this house."

CHAPTER 8

*N*oelle, Colorado
December 31, 1876

MINNIE GOLD GIGGLED, her voice echoing off the walls of
Madame Bonheur's bedroom. At first, the women had been
timid about entering the woman's room. However, they got
past that once they saw it was the nicest room in the house.
Minnie looked up at Fina's reflection in the large oval mirror
they stood in front of and laughed again. "I don't think I've
ever seen anyone so excited."

"Neither have I," said Birdie. "Now please stop moving so
I can finish this."

Fina commanded her feet to stay still. "I'm so sorry,
ladies. I'm just so excited… and nervous, too."

"Why?" Minnie asked. "I thought you said Nacho was 'la
crema en el café.'"

Fina laughed, enjoying how the woman's accent played
with the Spanish words. "He is and I'm sure that soon you'll
be finding the 'cream for your coffee,' too. Yes?"

She winked, but the hopeful bride waved her comment away. "Today isn't about me, dear. It's about you."

"Not quite," Birdie reminded them both. She pushed another pin into the fluffy dress. "She isn't getting married today. They're exchanging vows on… Fina, what did you call it again?"

"Día de Los Reyes," Josefina explained. "It's also known as Epiphany. It's when the three wise men visited the little baby Jesus in the manger and brought him wonderful gifts to celebrate his arrival."

"What a marvelous day to get married," Minnie gushed. "And with the little flowers I'm embroidering onto the dress, Mr. Villanueva is going to think *you* are the 'crema en el café.'"

The women giggled again and Birdie stood up.

"That should do it. You can go ahead and take it off now," she instructed Fina. "I'll get sewing straightaway and should have it done by tomorrow. Then I'll give it to Minnie to finish off."

"Yes, and it won't take me but a few hours to do the flowers. So, you should have the dress by tomorrow evening – certainly in enough time for your wedding day."

"That sounds wonderful. Thank you so much, ladies, for helping out. I know you've got your own lives to attend to – especially with you being newly married yourself, Birdie. Are you sure Mr. Peregrine won't mind?"

"Not at all. Jack knows how much I enjoy being a seamstress."

"Then if you insist—" Fina lifted her arms and waited for the women to pull the dress up over her head so she could slip out of it. Left standing in her cotton shift, she reached for the plain day dress draped across a chair. She grinned. "I guess it's back to this old thing until I exchange vows with Nacho. Speaking of which… I better hurry up and get down to the restaurant. I promised I would help with the dinner rush this evening."

"But that's not for hours," Minnie said.

"I know, but Nacho and I are decorating the restaurant before then. You wouldn't believe some of the beautiful paintings I found at his homestead. You ladies should definitely stop by!"

"If we did that, then we wouldn't finish the dress," Birdie joked.

"But I'm sure we'll be in eventually," Minnie added. "I love that sweet bread they serve up in the mornings."

"Then I'll be sure you both have the best piece waiting for you tomorrow," Josefina said as they bid their farewells. She finished dressing and took one more look in the mirror. Strands of hair had worked their way out of her usual braid. She did her best to pat them back into place and then slipped on her coat, ready to head down to the diner.

"My, don't you look quite the sight."

Fina spun around, glaring. The last person she wanted to see was Madame Bonheur.

"Don't worry. I was just leaving," Josefina said.

"Oh, I'm not worried at all, dear." The Madame gave her a smile that could only be described as the remnants of kindness after it had been thoroughly maimed and then killed. "You, on the other hand, should be."

Josefina rolled her eyes. "And why is that?"

"Well, I don't know about you, but I would be very concerned about my fiancé finding out I was no better than a common..." The Madame trailed off as she slowly walked around the room, straightening one knickknack after another. "Really, you girls have made such a mess here. Is this the kind of shambles you kept your room while entertaining clients?"

Josefina gasped. "I don't know what you're talking about."

111

"Oh, but your reaction tells me you do know… as did a little birdie." The Madame motioned to the air beside her head, her fingers fluttering as if a bird had just flown away.

Josefina gritted her teeth. "I was a dancing girl."

"Yes, I'm sure you were. Rather, I'm sure that's how you started out. You see, I've traveled all over this country and I specifically recall seeing a woman perform once – a woman who looked very much like you, Miss Fina. And her dancing? So similar to your own style that it could never be mistaken for any other. Now let me see," the Madame tapped her chin. "If I recall correctly, I do believe they introduced her as 'The Marvelous Maria.' Ring any bells?"

For the second time since her arrival in Noelle, Josefina felt ice in her veins.

"I can tell by the look on your face that it must," the Madame continued. "And if that much is right, then I'm sure it's equally true that you're still under contract… to a certain Mr. Hank Harvey of Hank's Whisky River Saloon. *Oui?*"

Josefina fell completely silent. She didn't know what to say. She could only manage to shake her head in denial.

"Come now. There's no point in lying about it. I've already spoken with the man myself. In fact, I've even seen the contract."

"But… how?"

A wicked grin slithered across the woman's face. "You should know better than anyone. Working women such as ourselves have always been good at keeping secrets."

Josefina slowly pieced together what the Madame was saying. "The strangers people have been talking about… the men… That's Hank and his men." She looked at the woman, incredulous. "They're staying with you!"

"Well, of course they are. With Seamus's saloon already full and this house still overrun with unwanted women, where else could they possibly stay? It didn't take long to find out what he was after once I got him and his men settled in."

"And what is it that he wants?"

Irritated, Madame Bonheur huffed. "Well, that's kind of obvious. You made him a lot of money."

"And what is it you want? Why are you telling me all this anyway?"

"Honestly? I couldn't care less if the man gets you back or not. However, I understand the sentiment of wanting revenge after something's been stolen from you. After all, no one likes their wallet being picked."

"I don't understand. I never took anything from you."

"No, you didn't. That's why I'm willing to make a little deal with you." The Madame brought herself to her full height and glared down at Josefina. "You didn't steal anything from me, but Nacho most certainly did. You see, Colette was one of *my* girls... and no one takes anything from me without eventually paying for it. So, you have a choice. I know full well that Nacho has a little stash of gold somewhere – Colette herself told me about it. You're going to get it for me as payment for losing one of my girls. In exchange, I'll keep the men tied up long enough for you to slip away out of town."

"What kind of plan is that?" Josefina asked, distraught. "I'm getting married next week."

Madame Bonheur laughed. "Do you really think he's going to marry you after he learns the truth?"

"Why not?" Josefina challenged. "As you already said – he married one of your girls."

"True, but the man knew what he was getting involved with from the beginning. She didn't lie about who she really was all the way up to her wedding day," the Madame crowed. "You, darling, are so much worse than a dancing girl or a whore. You're a lying one... with absolutely nothing to offer.

I mean, even Colette had a card to play with that pregnancy of hers – God only knows who the father really was. She saw right through Ignacio Villanueva, though. She knew he'd step right up to the responsibility of playing dear daddy. But you... you have none of that to offer the man. Now add thievery to the list. Do you really think he'll still marry you after you've stolen all his money, too?"

The room spun around Fina. She reached out and grabbed hold of the bed post to steady herself.

"Careful, my dear." Madame Bonheur feigned concern. "We wouldn't want you to lose that pretty little head of yours. At least, not until after we've carried out our plan. *Oui?*

Dazed, Josefina only nodded.

"Good," her rival responded. "I overheard your plan for when you wish to marry. So, you have until the day before then."

Madame Bonheur looked her up and down once and then shrugged, mumbling something about men having no taste as she left Fina standing there in the middle of the room, completely bewildered.

She numbly went about gathering her things to head out to the diner, her mind reeling. Surely there was something she could do to get out from under the Madame's thumb – not to mention Hank's – without betraying Ignacio in the process.

But what?

She was still rolling the question over in her mind as she departed *La Maison* and headed down the street, but was no closer to finding a solution when she finally reached her destination.

Nacho greeted her with a soft kiss on the hand. "Hola, chiquitita. I've been waiting all morning to see you. Come in out of the cold and I'll fix you something to eat."

Josefina passed through the entrance, waving away his offer. "I couldn't possibly eat anything right now."

He examined her with a look of concern. "You are not getting ill. Are you?

"No."

His apprehension heightened. "Are you getting nervous?"

"Nervous? What would I have to be nervous about?" she asked, fighting to keep the edge out of her voice.

"About the wedding. Is everything going well with the fitting? You know, it doesn't matter to me how you look when we get married. I think you're beautiful all the time."

"Ay, Nacho. You say the sweetest things." She looked away in an attempt to keep him from seeing the tears that had formed in the corner of her eyes. "It just that… well, look! This place isn't nearly finished and I was hoping to have it done before the dinner rush."

"That's no problem. It's still several hours before the first customer will arrive… and the pork is already simmering in a pot. We'll hang the rest of the paintings now and still be finished in enough time."

"But how? We don't even have all the paintings."

Confused, Nacho looked around the restaurant. "I'm sure I packed all of them. Which one is missing?"

"La Virgen."

"La Virgen? I thought you said that one had no business being in a restaurant. Too religious."

"I changed my mind," she explained. "With the new recipes and new year and everything else… Well, it's like a whole new business. *No crees?* Don't you think a new business needs a little blessing? Surely la Virgen looking down on us every day will do just that."

Nacho raised his hands, shrugging. "*Esta bien.* If that's what you want. I will ride out and pick it up right now."

"No need to trouble yourself. I can do it."

"Are you sure? First, you sprain your ankle and then you fall in the pond – not to mention that raccoon you had to fend off. Maybe it's not such a good idea for you to be venturing off by yourself. I wouldn't want anything to happen to you – especially with the wedding only a few days away."

"*No te preocupes. No pasa nada.*"

"It's hard for me to not worry, amor. Those things that happened weren't 'nothing' occurrences."

Determined, she crossed her arms and frowned. "*Por fa*, Ignacio. It's not like I'm going to be dancing around or trying to walk across the pond again. And I'm sure the raccoon is more afraid of me than I am of him by now. Besides, it's not like you can protect me from everything. I'm sure there will be plenty of occasions in the future when I'll have to make trips into town by myself – or remain at the homestead alone like the other night – and I'll make due just like I did then... The same as I always have. I hope you don't think that marrying you means you can start telling me what I can and cannot do."

"*Ya,* Fina. It's not that," he defended himself. "I was only showing my concern. I know you're more than capable of taking care of yourself. If it will make you that much happier, then go on and get the painting. I'll be here – hanging the rest of them. *De acuerdo?*"

"Thank you, Ignacio." She embraced him, a small feeling of guilt worming its way through her. She felt bad for using the opportunity to go search for the gold – *his* gold coins. It was the only time she would be alone to do so, though. She excused herself. "I'll return shortly."

He followed her outside, helping her climb into the buckboard and then bid farewell. She tried calculating how much time she had to get out to the homestead and search for the money before he started worrying about what was taking her so long.

This is wrong, her conscience gnawed at her. *What you're doing is terrible – and you know it.*

She tried to mentally shake away the thoughts echoing in her mind, but it was hard to deny the truth. No matter how much she tried to justify her actions, it didn't change the fact that she was not only lying to Nacho, but she was stealing from him as well.

"It won't be a lot," she whispered to herself. "I'll only take a few coins and tell Madame Bonheur that she'll have to make do with the little I could find. Then I'll still be free to marry Ignacio."

But what about Hank Harvey?

She mulled the question over her mind as she pulled up to the homestead and climbed out of the wagon. She hadn't been fortunate enough to have a copy of her contract with the saloon keeper, but there must have been some way out of it.

"I'll cross that bridge when I come to it," she mumbled and set out for the task at hand, entering the cabin to begin her search – so desperate to find the solution to her problems that she didn't even shut the door behind her. However, even the cold air that blustered in behind her wasn't enough to cool her hot pursuit of the money. Rationalizing that the raccoon had been downstairs when she first heard him, Fina figured that there was no need to search the bedrooms. Besides, she had already given both a thorough cleaning. Whatever the hiding spot was, it had to be in either the sitting room or the kitchen.

She searched around the living room first – breaking a light sweat as she ran her hands along the fireplace mantle, bent low to peer under the chairs and table, and knelt on the floor to feel along the carpet, inch by inch, for any secret trapped doors.

Secret trapped doors?

Josefina stood and groaned.

"Estás loca? You can't do this! What are you thinking?"

She plopped down in one of the chairs, burying her head in her hands. Madame Bonheur was right. If she took even a single coin, then there really wouldn't be any future with Nacho. Why hadn't she trusted him to begin with? Maybe he would have understood. Maybe they could have—

She felt her chair suddenly tip back. A hand on her shoulder firmly clamped down on her.

"Wha—"

She turned just as the other large, calloused hand of a strange man clamped down over her mouth, thwarting her attempt to scream. Her feet left the ground as she was pulled right up out of the chair.

"Hello, Fina." A deep voice commanded her attention. She turned her head what little she could and Hank came into view. He glowered at her, his long, auburn mane falling over his shoulder, making him look like a lion ready to attack. "I've been looking all over for you."

He motioned to the man holding her and he released her. She stared at him, shocked into silence.

"Well, aren't you going to say hello?" he asked, feigning a friendly character.

Josefina swallowed past the lump in her throat. "Hello, Hank."

The man clucked his tongue at her. "Aw, come on now. You can do better than that. Can't you?"

He quickly grabbed her and pulled her close enough for her to smell his morning booze lingering on his breath. She turned her head just as he lowered his, missing her lips to

THE DANCING LADY

plant a rough kiss on her cheek. He glared at her with disgust. "You know, you used to welcome my kisses."

Finally finding her voice, she turned back to him. "That was before you started selling me out. Remember?"

"Hey, you didn't have it so bad," he said. "Not like some of the other women... Remember?"

He gave her a slick, sick smile that made her stomach churn. "I'm not like the other women."

"You're right. You're not. That's why I rode all the way out here with my men to find you." He sighed and dug into his pocket to pull out a cigar. He bit the end of it and spit it out onto the floor beside the hearth. The man that had grabbed her rummaged about in his own pocket and pulled out a match. He lit it and then held it out for Hank. The man puffed on his stogy until the end turned cherry red. He blew out a thick cloud of smoke. "You've cost me a lot of coin, Fina. Money you'll have to pay back somehow. In fact, I was here the other night to collect. I saw that Mexican fella leave and thought it might have been the perfect time to enter, but then I heard all kinds of thrashing going on and remembered how wild you could get sometimes."

Hank stepped close to her and lowered his face close to hers. He gently ran the tip of his nose across her cheek, taking in deep breaths of her fragrance. "I can't help but wonder if you're as wild for him as you were for me."

He straightened up again and took another puff. As if suddenly bored, he motioned to the man again. "Alright. Take her on out."

"Wait!" Josefina frantically cries. "Let me go... and I'll buy out my own contract."

Hank studied her for a moment, slightly amused. Then he snorted. "You gonna buy out your contract? How you gonna to do that? You could hardly work it off when you were still with me. Now you suddenly came into a fortune or something?"

He laughed and the other man joined in.

"Almost," she lied.

"Oh, yeah?" Still amused, Hank took a drag off his cigar. The smoke snaked out through his half-smiling lips. "What kind of money we talking about?"

"Big money," she continued, wondering if she was ever going to live the kind of life that wasn't built on one false-hood after another. "Like the kind of money a man could live on for the rest of his life."

Hank stared at her for a moment, one eye squinting in disbelief. "Hey, you're not trying to play me. Are you? Because you know that would be real dangerous, Fina, and you're already in a heap of trouble for running off to begin with."

Josefina summoned all her courage. "And you know me better than to think I'd lie about money."

He stroked the stubble growing in on his chin. "Yeah, I used to think I did. Then you up and ran off."

She shrugged. "What did you expect, Hank? You've heard me talk about my family before – the desire to find my father and sister. When I learned about this mail order bride busi-ness, I figured I'd see how I could cash in."

A sly smile slinked across Hank's expression, making him look even more like the treacherous serpent he rightly was. "And now you're thinking of cashing in big, are you?"

"I am. Rather, I will when we marry on *El Día de Los Reyes.*"

"What the heck is that?"

"The day of Epiphany."

"Well, when is it?"

"January sixth."

He considered her proposal for a moment, pacing the

room as he continued to smoke his cigar. He stopped in front of the painting of the Virgin hanging on the living room wall. "Alright," he finally said. "Go get this money you say you've got and I'll let you out of your contract."

"It doesn't work like that," Josefina said. "I have to marry the guy first. That way I have a right to the money and he can't set the law after me for taking it. After all, a man wouldn't have his own wife arrested."

"I suppose not," Hank agreed. "A man don't like to be embarrassed in front of his friends. It would be bad for a business that's already struggling."

Josefina raised a curious brow and Hank shrugged. "I've heard things."

His simple explanation made it obvious that Madame Bonheur had shared more than her bed with the man – another account Fina would have felt bad about had she not thought the man deserved whatever came his way. She pushed the thought aside and plowed on. None of that was her business – the same as it wasn't Hank's business that the diner was sure to see better days with the new recipes and decor.

"Well, the way I figure it is that I'll go through with the vows and then I'll have legal access to the money. As soon as I do, I'll hand it over to you – in exchange for the contract, of course."

"Of course," Hank said and flicked ashes on the carpet. "But you must think I'm dumb to not see you really want to marry this Mexican fella of yours. What happened Fina? Find a man to finally match that fiery heart of yours?" He snorted at her discomfort. "Don't worry. You'll get what you want. So's long as I get what I want."

"You will," she said.

"I better... or I'll let that man and everyone else in town know exactly who and what you are," he promised. "But come through with the money and I'll quietly slip away. We have an understanding?"

Josefina nodded.

"Good. Then you better get on out of here and get to it."

She hurriedly did as he suggested and stumbled out onto the porch, past yet another hired hand, and down to the wagon. She swiftly scrambled up it to take her seat, silently cursing herself for allowing the man to run her out of her own home. Well, what would eventually become her home if everything worked out the way she hoped it would.

She glanced back only momentarily to see Hank hovering in the doorway, a serious scowl on his face. For as sure as she was that he would clean up after himself (or have his men do so) before leaving the homestead, she was equally certain that he would never let her go. Would he try to find a way to get the money before she married... or wait until she had exchanged vows and take her anyway? She couldn't guarantee which scenario would play out, but one thing was clear. Hank Harvey wasn't about to let any woman of his simply walk away.

Especially one that had embarrassed him or made his business suffer.

She drove on towards town, her mind reeling with how wrong things had turned. How was she to get out from under the fabrications she had told? A pack of lies that were to grow by at least one more when yet another fact struck her.

She had forgotten the painting.

CHAPTER 9

N̸oelle, CO
January 1, 1877

"YOU'RE GOING OUT *NOW?*" Josefina set the dirty dishes back down on the table and scowled. "It's nearly ten o'clock at night!"

"I know what time it is," Nacho groused.

"Then why are you going out?"

"I need some fresh air."

"Fresh air?" Josefina threw her arms up. "You'll find the same air in here that you'll find outside."

He ignored her and shoved his arms in his coat.

"What about closing down the restaurant?" she continued. "We've hardly begun cleaning up, let alone preparing for tomorrow."

"Then leave it," he said and stormed to the front door. Worried, Josefina followed him.

"But how am I to get back to the house? What if I get tired and start to fall asleep?"

He almost told her to go back to *La Maison*, but quickly reminded himself he wasn't upset enough to send her packing – just upset that she was hiding something. "You know there's a room back there with a bed in it. If I'm not back soon, then take it."

"But where will you sleep?"

"Wherever I please."

Her gasp made him feel a little guilty. He was being unfair and he knew it. Still, he couldn't bring himself to look at her. Seeing her upset would make him change his mind and he was tired of her playing him like a fool.

Like a lovesick one.

"Depending on the time, I'll either sleep on the floor out here or make my way back to the homestead," he called over his shoulder and then slammed the door for emphasis. Her cry could be heard clear through to the other side and it almost made him turn back.

Not this time, he chided himself. He wouldn't be duped again. She was lying to him about something – that much was clear – and it was no way to begin a marriage. Either the situation would be resolved or there would be no vows.

He racked his mind, trying to figure out what she was about. He hated to think what the possibilities were, but they didn't look good. He had noticed some strange occurrences after she returned emptyhanded from her ride out the day before. Her uneasy behavior followed by their drive home to the distinct smell of a Cuban cigar... It all reminded him too much of Colette and the rumors he now knew to be true. Was that what had happened with Fina? Had another man found his way into her heart? Wormed him way into her bed? And right after he had sent the wire hiring a Pinkerton agent to find her family?

The idea made him sick.

He pushed through Seamus's bar, surprised to see the tree

some men had previously found already decorated. Small grays hung on them, but he gave them only a moment's notice.

He took a seat at the bar. "Pour me one, amigo."

Seamus eyed him for a moment. "You're not drinking again, are ya, man? You're to be married in a few days. It's not fitting."

"Please, Seamus. I need the drink – not one of your lectures right now."

The barkeep frowned but did as requested, filling a mug with some rotgut and sliding it in front of Nacho. "Well, if you want to talk about it instead…"

Nacho stared at the mug for a moment and then looked around to see who might be listening. Thankfully, the place wasn't as full as usual and the likelihood of eavesdropping was slim. He leaned towards Seamus, motioning for the man to come closer.

"I think Josefina might be two timing me," he muttered.

Seamus gave him a crazy eyed look. "Come now, man. You don't really believe that," he scoffed.

Nacho ran his hands over his face, rubbing his tired eyes. "I don't know. I can't figure out what else she might be hiding."

"Why does she have to be hiding anything at all? You know how woman are – confusing sometimes."

"It's not that," Nacho insisted. "I know she's hiding something, Seamus… and I won't be conned the same way I was with Colette. Not again."

"Well, did you ask her what was wrong? Did you try that yet? Maybe it's not her at all. Maybe it's you."

"Me?" Nacho sat back, exasperated. "What have I done?"

"Well, I don't know. You expect a woman to come in here and start cooking for you like it's a natural calling – which I guess it might be for some, but I'm not so sure with your lady friend. I've heard some tales that she could probably spin in perfect circles better than she can stir a pot."

"Who's spreading such stories?" Nacho demanded.

"Just one or two of the guys talking about things they've overheard from their wives."

"The new brides?"

Seamus nodded.

"Which ones?"

"Sorry, friend. Ya know I don't go dropping names like that. Besides, maybe it isn't true. I'm only asking you to consider the possibility. After all, those women were the ones all traveling and living together. It would be no surprise if they knew more about each other than we did. Even if that isn't the problem, though, have you made yourself approachable so she can talk to you... or has it mostly been all about you?"

Nacho snorted. Sure, he had shared some about himself and asked her to learn his mother's recipes. What was so wrong with that? It wasn't all about him or his diner, though. He had found out about her family. Hadn't he? So, maybe it had taken a few days and maybe it hadn't been entirely planned. Alright. It hadn't been planned at all. Still, it wasn't like *all* their time had been discussing recipes. Well, not all of it. Sometimes they talked about his family and *their* lives – like his father's painting and his brothers ranching. They talked about his homestead, too, and his past with Colette and...

He slapped his forehead. "*Ay, por la gracia de Dios.* You're right, Seamus. I've spent so much time telling her about me that I haven't really gotten to know about her. Even when the opportunity presented itself, there was only once that I actually took the initiative – and that was done because I was afraid of being lied to more than anything."

"Sounds like it's time you go and get to know your bride a little better."

"Past time," Nacho agreed. He pushed the drink forward. "Guess I won't be needing this after all. Thanks, Seamus."

He stood and left the saloon, choosing not to head straightaway to the diner. He had to think first. Walking up and down the main street of Noelle, he slowly strolled past the buildings while considering Seamus's suggestion. Was it possible that Josefina really knew nothing about cooking? How could that be? He had been over to *La Maison* on three different occasions when she had cooked specifically for him. In fact, one had been the most delicious apple pie he had ever tasted. That one hadn't even been in his mother's recipe book! Unless...

Could it be that she wasn't the one really cooking the meals? No, that wasn't it. The other two meals were strictly Mexican meals his mother use to make. It wouldn't have been possible for any of the other ladies to know the recipes. Perhaps others had been helping her before that – giving her advice on the basics.

The more he thought about it, the more sense it made. She didn't seem very comfortable around the kitchen – always waiting for him to take the lead, or choosing to wait on the customers more than help in the kitchen. He originally thought she was simply trying to get to know everyone in town, but now he wasn't so sure. It could have all been a ploy to avoid being in the kitchen.

He came full circle and stopped in front of the diner, looking up at the sign that hung above it. Only a dim light shone through one window, implicating that she had finished in the front room and was somewhere in the back. He entered the diner, hopeful she wasn't yet asleep because both his mind and heart were full.

And he was determined to find out everything he could about his bride-to-be.

~

JOSEFINA FIDDLED with one of the red roses on the wedding dress. Minnie had done a fabulous job embroidering them. Their delicate little petals and stems decorated the hem of the dress like a border in a flower patch. She sighed and let the dress fall back against the dressing screen – the place she had put it when Minnie dropped it off earlier that morning… when things had been much calmer and far more joyous. Now here she was arguing with Nacho, watching him storm out into the night.

What a difference half a day could make!

She walked over to the bed and fell into it, saddened by the day's turn of events. She knew she had no one to blame but herself, though. She only had four days left to make her deadline for both the Madame and Hank. The one wouldn't allow her to marry unless she found the money… and suggested that she wouldn't be wanted anyway. The other wanted her to marry specifically for the money… but probably still would have tried to cart her off. Then there was the matter of her own guilty conscience of not wanting to take any of Nacho's money anyway – not that she even knew where it was.

This was simply too much!

She turned her head into the pillow and let out a wretched sob. She was exhausted of trying to always be strong. All the strength in the world was no match for the weight of so much deception. If she could be certain Nacho wouldn't cast her aside like an old hat, she would tell him everything. She wouldn't wait a minute longer, either. She would tell him *right now.*

"Why are you crying?"

Josefina shot up, but refused to turn around. She sat at the edge of the bed, wiping away her tears and shrugged. "I'm not crying."

Nacho sighed and strode across the room to sit on the opposite side of the bed. He reached out and laid a hand on her shoulder, giving it a gentle squeeze. "You don't have to act so tough all the time. That's why you have me – so we can be stronger together. However, that's not going to happen if we don't trust one another."

Her head hanged. "You're not the one who has the problem trusting people."

"That's not true. I do have a problem with that."

She twisted towards him, her face contorted with confusion. "How? You've trusted me with many things. You let me borrow your mother's book. You lent me the horse and wagon to go out to the house. I think it suffices to say that if anything, you have been far more generous than I."

"Fina, those are just *things*. Sure, I would have been disappointed if anything happened to them, but that doesn't change the fact that I didn't trust *you* as a whole."

Her head dropped with shame. "Perhaps because I haven't given you much reason to."

"Eh," Nacho wavered. "That might hold a little truth to it. You see, I know that you're hiding something. I don't know exactly what it is, but it's obvious that it's something serious. So, why don't you tell me what it is? Hopefully, it will be much better than my unfounded fears that you've fallen for someone else."

Her eyes widened. "I would never! Nacho, I love—"

She clamped her mouth shut. It wasn't right for her to profess such feelings after all the hurt she was willing to cause him.

"What were you saying?" He gave her a large grin. "Come now, let us begin telling truths. Yes? You said you love—"

"Your cooking," she said and turned up her nose. "Are you satisfied? I love your cooking."

"Oh, how wonderful... because, you know, I love your little *salchichas*."

She let out a small indignant yelp. "I do not have sausage toes!"

He threw his head back and a throaty laugh escaped. She slapped his arm which made him laugh even harder. When she failed to see the humor in it all, he wrapped his arms around her and pulled her close, quieting some. "Don't be like that, amor. Say you feel the same for me as I feel for you. I know I haven't done the best to show it – always talking about me and what I want—"

"Yes, and always teasing me."

"Aw, that's just my way of showing that I care. If you really don't like me doing it, then I won't."

She gave him a guilty look. "I guess I don't mind it so much – as long as it isn't about my feet. I know they are kind of squared. That's from years of practice, though."

"From dancing?"

She nodded. "Yes, because I used to dance."

"Tell me more," he encouraged her. "I want to know everything. How you learned to dance... when you did it. Everything."

"Well, I guess you could say it all started with my mother. She was trained in several styles of dance..."

Josefina continued on, revealing her mother's growing desire to become renowned and the separation that grew between her parents. The next thing she knew, she was spilling out *most* of the truths of her sordid past. She told him about dancing for Hank and both the man and Madame Bonheur trying to finagle money out of her – *his* money.

"I wasn't going to do it, though. I had already made up my mind that tomorrow I was going to tell them the arrangements were off."

He suddenly stood and strode out of the room.

Fearful he was thoroughly repulsed by her past, she raced after him. "Nacho, please forgive me. I'm so sorry."

"There is nothing to forgive," he said as he entered the dining room and pulled the gun out from its hidden spot from behind the counter.

"Ignacio! What are you doing with that thing?"

"I'm going to find the sheriff... and then to have a serious discussion with la Señora Bonheur and find this no good Hank you speak of. I will teach them to try to intimidate *my* fiancé. They'll both be sitting in a jail cell by the time we're finished."

"Wait," Fina cried. "You can't do that."

"Why not? I will not bear that woman meddling in my affairs any longer. She has been a thorn in every single person's backside for as long as I can remember. It's time she understood that certain things will not be tolerated in this town – blackmail being one of them."

"But what about Hank?"

"What do I care about this man and his silly piece of paper? He wants to see you dance? We'll put on a show for dinner one night."

She hung her head, her voice filled with dismay. "You don't understand. I was more than his dancing girl."

Nacho carefully approached her. He laid the pistol on the counter beside where she stood. "Fina, what is it you're not telling me?"

She choked back a cry, forcing herself to meet his gaze. This was the moment she had been waiting for – the one where she would follow through with her promise to stop subsisting with a life full of lies. Whatever happened next would be up to him to decide.

"Dancing didn't earn me enough to survive," she declared. "I did what I had to do – the same as the women of *La Maison de Chats*. You had asked the agency for 'a God-fearing woman' who knew how to cook and sew. I'm sorry to say I'm not that woman, though. I thought you should know that before you make the mistake of rushing off to defend my honor. I have none left."

His confused expression forced her to finally look away, her heart breaking at the sudden awareness that she no longer had a future with Nacho. Perhaps she never really did.

He finally spoke. "Is that all you have to say?"

Her head snapped back up. Not trusting her voice, she only nodded.

"Good. Then I'll do as I stated earlier and go for the sheriff."

"But what about everything I just told you?" She sighed heavily. "What about all the lies?"

A smallest trace of a smirk pulled at his friendly face. "*Ay, mi fina* Fina. You know, you really shouldn't confuse a calm demeanor with ignorance. Everything you just confessed? I kind of already knew."

"You did? But how?"

"Well, you see, I'm not exactly the greatest cook in the world. I have the desire for it, but until I got a hold of my mother's recipes, I didn't have a whole lot of skill. Still, there are a few dishes I do know how to make, and one of them is beans. Truth is, yours were even worse than mine."

She gasped.

"Sorry, amor. I mean no offense. I'm only saying that it doesn't get much simpler than that. The fact you didn't know how to make even those caused me to question how well you knew how to cook at all, but I kept making excuses – especially after seeing you dedicate yourself to learning my mother's recipes. Every time I came over for a visit, you tried a little something new, surprising me with a dish I didn't expect. That's when I convinced myself all that mattered was that you had the same desire as me. I see now that it isn't entirely true. Is it?"

Fina glanced away.

"Not exactly." His disappointed sigh made her rush on. "But nothing would make me happier than to see your dream come true of making 'Nacho's Tacos' the finest dining establishment in all of Noelle."

He beamed brightly. "Truly?"

"Of course. I saw how content you were on your visits to *La Maison* when I brought you a hot meal. I would love to make that a part of my daily routine."

"Maybe not every day. Don't forget that I, too, enjoy cooking. I would like to return the favor sometimes. Besides, there are other things that I know you enjoy doing as well. Things that I think should become a part of your daily routine... as well as an established part of the restaurant."

"You mean my dancing?"

"*Claro.* We could host something called 'Fancy Fridays' where folks from all around come to see your beautiful dancing while they enjoy a magnificent meal."

"You would do that for me?"

"Of course. I, too, enjoy seeing you happy."

"But what about the rest of it?" she asked, referring to the way she had earned a living. "You aren't angry that I lied about what I did."

"To be honest? I was very upset while you were saying it. Not so much about what you did or the idea that you couldn't find any other way to make money, but more because you lied about it. Then I remembered the not-so-small detail that I don't have a squeaky-clean past myself.

How can I judge you for doing what you had to survive, when I was the sort of man supporting that kind of work? Furthermore, it is in the past. The important thing for us to remember as we move forward is to always be honest with one another, as well as take the time to listen."

Now that the truth was finally out, Fina felt a great weight lift off her shoulders. Now that they were making amends with each other – and their pasts – they could have a fresh start and begin again. She gave him a warm smile. "Thank you for understanding, Nacho. I'm so thankful we can start all over as friends."

"*Cómo?* Woman, I'm not starting all over again. I mean, we're going to be friends, yes… but we're getting married, too. Now that's final." His eyes widened and he smiled. "Hey, that's a good idea. Why don't we get married right now?"

"Get married *now?*"

"Think about it. There's no way your contract with him would hold any water against a marriage contract. No judge would rule in his favor – not that I think it would even go that far. I don't think any decent folks here in town would stand for it. And now that I know the truth, the blackmail for money won't work for him… or la Señora Bonheur. So, the sooner we marry, the better."

She giggled. "You're insane."

"Perhaps." He drew her close, his dark eyes full of desire. "They say love will make a man do crazy things."

"The same is true for a woman," she agreed right before his mouth covered hers. The kiss deepened, making her mind and body reel. He gently pulled away, leaving her lips still aching with passion.

"Now go get your dress."

"But what about the Reverend? It must be midnight by now. Surely he's asleep. And where will we marry anyway?"

"Don't worry about a thing. Everything will work out perfectly, but we have to hurry."

Filled with nervous excitement, she raced off to the back room and grabbed her garments, returning a minute later to find him waiting with her coat in hand.

"You're not wearing the dress."

"Of course not. It's bad luck for the groom to see the bride before her wedding."

"Now don't you go picking up any of that superstitious stuff like your friend – the one who thinks she has bad luck."

It had been a few days since she'd seen Penny, but Josefina hadn't stopped thinking about her. She hoped the woman was doing well and that her misfortunes had subsided. She ignored the comment. "I'm sure there will be a place for me to get ready wherever we're going. Where is it anyway?"

"Not far." Nacho escorted her out of the diner, placing a handmade sign in the window announcing they were closed. Then he locked the door behind them. "I've learned my lesson about leaving the place unlocked. You never know who might wander in."

Having heard the story about Grandpa Gus, Fina laughed. "I doubt we'll have that problem at this hour of the night."

"You're right. Now let's hurry before Seamus closes."

She followed him down the street. "We're going to the saloon?"

"Yes. It's a saloon. Seamus stays up pretty late trying to convince the stragglers to go to bed. Besides, the Reverend and his new wife stay in one of the rooms above the bar. So, he won't have to travel far to marry us."

"You're right. He would be doing us a great favor," Josefina agreed. She lifted the dress a little higher as they trudged through the snow, thankful when they finally reached the bar and saw that the place was still lit. They entered to find Seamus trying to shake the drink out of Elmer Copperpot.

"Come, man. Ya know ya can't sleep here. Pull on out." He looked up, dismayed to see Nacho. "What are *you* doing back here? I thought—"

He spied a fluffy cream-colored garment and cranked his head to find Fina standing behind her groom-to be.

"My apologies, ma'am. I didn't see you standing there." He raised a questioning brow at Nacho who raised his hands in defense. "Don't worry, *amigo*. We're only here to ask the Reverend to marry us."

"*Now?*"

"It's a long story, but yes. Now."

Seamus shrugged. "Alright. Well, you know which room is his. I guess you can just go on up and see if you can wake him. I've got to get the rest of these laggards off."

"Come on," Nacho said to Fina as Seamus attempted to once again wake Elmer. "Maybe you can use his room to change into the dress."

She followed him upstairs, trying to calm her excitement as he knocked on the Reverend's door. After a couple of minutes, it finally swung open.

"Nacho? What are you doing here?"

"We want to get married?"

"Right now?" the Reverend asked with astonishment. "It's only... wait a minute. What time *is* it anyway?"

Nacho dug into his pocket and pulled out a watch. He flipped it open. "A quarter after midnight."

"Nacho! Can't this wait until the morning?"

"See, here's the thing..." Nacho proceeded to tell the Reverend the shortened version of the troubles he and Fina faced. "So, you see that the sooner we get married, the better."

"And not just for us," Josefina chimed in. "Our marriage will be one more to add to the list so the train will come to Noelle."

"Yes, let's not forget about that," Nacho agreed. "After all, that's why we sent off for the brides to begin with. Right?"

"Oh, do it, Chase." Felicity suddenly appeared, fully dressed. "Let's go downstairs and marry them right away."

His wife's enthusiasm made the Reverend smile. "I'll need a minute to get dressed."

"As will I," Josefina said and held up the dress. "If you don't mind, of course."

"Not at all. Just give me a minute to ready myself and then I'll leave you and Felicity to do the same."

He excused himself and true to his word reappeared a few minutes later. He invited Josefina in and left, shutting the door behind him, but not before she heard the man joke about a month of free meals at the restaurant in exchange for the midnight call.

Felicity shook her head. "He isn't serious."

"I'm sure Nacho wouldn't mind even if he was." She slipped out of her old dress and held up her arms as Felicity helped her into the wedding gown. "You are both doing us such a great favor."

"It's nothing at all," her friend insisted. "I can't think of anything I dislike more than a woman being blackmailed. As soon as you're married, I'm sure Sherriff Draven will have no problem running that Hank fellow out of town and having a heart-to-heart with Madame Bonheur. The nerve of some people. They seem to forget that women have rights, too. *All* women."

Josefina smiled up at her friend, remembering how she had been involved in some kind of suffragette movement in her hometown. "You're right, of course. How wonderful to find strong men who don't mind equally strong women."

"Exactly. Now that should do it. Turn around and let me see you."

Josefina did as instructed. "What do you think?"

"You look perfect. The dress suits you."

"Thank you," Josefina said. "After all the work they did, I wish Birdie and Minnie could have seen me in it."

"Maybe they still can."

"What do you mean? We couldn't possibly wake them now."

"No, but don't you enjoy dancing? Maybe you could dance in it sometime – like a reenactment or something."

"What a lovely idea. I'll suggest that to Nacho after we exchange vows."

"Then what are we waiting for?"

The two women rushed downstairs to find the men waiting beside the Christmas tree.

"I thought we could get married right here," Nacho explained. "Look. It even has a little dancing lady on it."

Josefina ran a finger down the porcelain ornament. "How sweet. Did you do this?"

"No," Nacho admitted. "However, I think it's very fitting. Don't you?"

She smiled up at him, eyes full of love. "I do."

"I do, too," Nacho whispered and leaned in to kiss her.

"Oh, Lord." Elmer Copperpot finally arose from the place he had dozed off. He stalked out of the saloon, muttering. "I ain't sticking around for none of this mush."

Of course, Nacho and Fina were too busy to hear anything else he had to say. The Reverend finally tapped Nacho on the shoulder.

"Eh hem," he cleared his throat. "I think you're supposed to wait to do that until after I marry the two of you."

Nacho laughed. "Then say the vows, amigo. This one has swift feet. I don't want her getting away."

"They would only find their way right back to you," Josefina promised as she took Nacho's hand in hers to recite their vows. When the Reverend finally pronounced them "man and wife," Nacho leaned forward again and kissed her so thoroughly that it made her heart beat a new rhythm. He finally pulled away, leaving her a bit heady. "Kiss me like that again and I won't be able to walk – let alone dance."

Her husband let out a throaty laugh and scooped her up, cradling her in his arms. "Don't worry, amor. You have a most willing partner now... and I will never let you fall again. So long as you are mine, of course."

With a look of love radiating in her eyes, she answered truthfully, "I would sacrifice a thousand dances in any life if only to love you forever in this one. Now kiss me again."

And he did.

EPILOGUE

 *wo weeks later...*

JOSEFINA LIFTED the spoon from her bowl and blew on it. Now was the moment of truth. Was this attempt finally going to yield the perfect pot of *pozole*? The pork had to be tender, the vegetables plentiful and the hominy thoroughly cooked. She wanted it to be ready and waiting for Nacho when he returned from his business in town. She took a small bite of the stew, savored it for a moment and then turned back to the pot to add a dash more salt.

"There," she said. "That should be perfect."

Nacho quietly entered the kitchen and slid up behind her.

"I'm sure it is," he said and she jumped.

"You scared me."

He gave her an impish grin and wrapped his arms around her. "What have you got to be scared of? The sheriff ran that no account and his men out of town. The Madame is no longer a threat either. See? You are completely safe."

He planted a kiss on the top of her head and she relaxed into his arms.

"You're right, of course. That's why I made the *pozole*. Now that we're truly free to do so without any strife, I want us to really celebrate our new life together."

"That's not all we're going to be celebrating." Nacho pulled back and produced a telegram from one of his pockets. He handed it to her. "I've been waiting a while for this. It finally arrived today."

"What is it?"

"You tell me. Go on and read it."

She unfolded the paper and read its message. Then she clutched it to her chest, breathless with excitement. "Is this real?"

Nacho grinned wildly. "I told you I would help find your family."

"Yes, but a Pinkerton agent?" She squealed with delight and then caged her excitement again. "I've seen the books, Nacho. We can't possibly afford all the things we want to do with the diner and pay for a Pinkerton, too."

"Amor, the money from the business is separate from my own savings. I thought you realized that when you found the raccoon with the coin."

"That was yours?"

"Of course."

"But I don't understand. How did the raccoon get it?"

Nacho rubbed the back of his neck, a grimace turning into a sheepish grin. "So the way I figured it was that everyone keeps their money hidden in their house, because the town doesn't have a bank. That being common practice, I reasoned that I didn't want anyone trying to break into my home. Therefore, I decided to keep the money somewhere *outside* the house."

"So, where did you keep it?"

"Remember that large tree out front? Well, it's empty inside. At least that's what I thought."

Josefina giggled. "You hid the money in a tree?"

"It seemed like a good idea at the time."

She laughed even harder. "Well, I hope you've moved it since then."

"I had to," he explained. "I needed to pay for the telegram, as well as a deposit for the agent to begin searching for your family."

"Is this really happening?" Josefina asked, her excitement once again building at the thought of seeing her father and sister, Elena. "It feels like a delicious dream come true."

Nacho chuckled. "Delicious? Now you're speaking my language. Let's eat!"

She moved to the stove and prepared two bowls of the pozole. Then she set them on the table. Adoration filled Nacho's eyes at the sight of a familiar childhood meal. He took a bite and smiled. "It tastes just like *mi mama* used to make."

"I hope so. I used her recipe."

Nacho beamed with pride. "Have I told you how much I love you?"

"Perhaps, but I won't complain if you tell me once again."

His expression filled with passion. "*Te amo más que una estrella fugaz que baila en el cielo nocturno.*"

The comparison that she was as beautiful as a falling star dancing across the night sky warmed her heart, and she knew for certain then.

It was going to be a delicious life.

AFTERWORD

Thank you so much for taking this journey with me to Noelle, Colorado. Out of all the stories I've written yet, *The Dancing Lady* is by far one of my favorites. Josefina and Ignacio seemed destined to fall in love. Then again, most of my characters usually do.

That raises a question, though. What about Josefina's younger sister? Will Elena find her happily ever after, too? I invite you to keep turning the pages and travel with me to the captivating country of Spain to find out what happens to her. Also, please enjoy a scene from the next book, *The Lord* by Danica Favorite, in this *12 Days of Christmas Mail Order Bride* series. If you enjoy these stories, then I welcome you to connect with me online to stay up-to-date with all my stories and other happenings at any of the following:

www.mimimilan.com
www.facebook.com/MimiMilanBooks
www.twitter.com/thewritingMimi

https://www.bookbub.com/authors/mimi-milan
https://www.amazon.com/Mimi-Milan/e/B011O65CQU/

Again, thank you so much for reading.

Chau!

Dear Miss Minnie Gold,

I like the sound of your name, especially if it brings real gold back to our town. Though I will consider having you as my bride my greatest treasure. Perhaps you think I speak too boldly, given that we have not yet met. But a woman who is willing to marry a man with nothing to offer but his name and his talents is a treasure indeed.

I'm told women appreciate poetry, but I lack the skill with words, so I hope you will instead accept my sincere wish for us to build a life together. In time, perhaps the deep abiding love romanticized through the ages will come. But even if it does not, I pledge to you my faithfulness, loyalty, and respect. These qualities are important to me, so I pray you will offer me the same.

I cannot provide you a vast estate or wealth beyond measure, but I believe true wealth resides in a man's heart and home. So perhaps I can offer that to you after all. As for material things, I am an assayer. A simple description is that when the miners find gold or other precious minerals, I test them to see what they are, and what their value might be. It's been a while since I've had the privilege of telling our townspeople that we have gold, but we're all hopeful that will change soon.

I don't know what else to tell you. I'm handsome enough, I suppose. I haven't scared anyone off with my looks, so that should count for something. I take a man at his word, and I don't tolerate liars. If you should arrive in Noelle and find me lacking, there will be no hard feelings as long as you are honest with me. I suspect it will take time for us to become comfortable with one another, and though I would like children in the future, I am in no hurry, so rest assured that those things will be resolved in due course.

I look forward to meeting you, and that we can build a companionable life together in Noelle.

I am, your servant,

Hugh Montgomery

Continue Reading *The Lord* by Danica Favorite.

Of all the rotten luck!

"You don't understand. I *am* the daughter of Vicente de Zapatero."

The guards threw back their heads with laughter.

"And I'm the bloody Count del Castillo," one wheezed with mirth.

Elena firmly planted both fists on her hips. "You mock me, sir. However, I speak the truth. If you would only go inside and—"

"Now see here, you foul little *zorra*..."

Elena gasped.

"... We've had enough with the likes of you. The *fiesta* is by invitation only. Unless you can produce one, you're not getting in. Neither are the rest of the wanton workers who keep wandering this way. The Count wants a wife – not whatever disease you and your ilk obviously carry. Now get out of here before we arrest you!"

Elena bit back a retort. The last thing she wanted was to land in a *carcel*, trapped behind thick iron bars set in solid stone. She gathered her skirts with a distinct *"humph"* and gave the guards one last glare before moving along. She wandered away, waiting until she had rounded the corner and was free to feel along the tall stone wall.

There has to be another way in!

Yet the only thing in view was a lush orange tree, its branches heavy with ripe fruit. She had heard tales of the trees surrounding the House of Castillo. It was common knowledge that on the day of "Passing the Peerage," the superseding noble was to authorize a new law. Typically, it was something that taxed the villagers and they were required to give a greater portion of their grain or donate livestock. Naturally, there would be quiet complaints amongst the townsfolk – criticisms that would die on the tips of their tongues before reaching the powerful nobility who could create costlier, even fatal conditions. However, such had not been the case with the last señor. In a moment of rare generosity, the late Conde del Castillo had ordered the trees planted in an attempt to feed the poorest of the villagers. Each family was allowed one orange apiece, encouraged to sow the seeds and nurture the soil it claimed, the hope being that it would eventually take root.

Hence the explanation of this sole climber standing like an unwounded soldier loaded with ammunition. Elena leaned against it, welcoming the cool shade its canopy offered. She slowly slid down the trunk, plopping onto the cool grass below with a soft thud. The moment's rest gave her time to examine her bare feet, bloody and sore from the long walk into town. If she thought they looked bad now, she could only manage what was to be expected once the blisters turned into callouses. She grimaced. Oh, well. They would look terrible, but at least she had saved the shoes. Smiling, she patted the hidden pocket sewn in her skirt, proud of the little secret held there. She glanced around, ensuring there were no witnesses present. When all appeared safe, she reached into the pouch and pulled out one of the delicate slippers. Encrusted with precious jewels her father had spent years to procure, it gleamed in the sun like a promise.

Better days awaited her.

She carefully balanced the shoe in one hand, bringing it close to her face so she could examine the intricate pattern designed so that each gem would catch and reflect the maximum amount of light imaginable. She had to admit that while she was a good shoemaker, she had yet to obtain the craftsmanship her father had effortlessly produced. The thought of him and the news she was to deliver to her step-mother brought on an episode of fresh tears. Openly weeping, she clutched the slipper to her chest, intent on having herself a good cry until the snapping sound of a branch overhead caused her to look up.

"Hola, hermosa."

Elena screamed, the outcry startling a man poised on one

slender branch, his arms desperately flapping up and down. However, the more he flailed the weaker his balance grew until he, predictably, landed with a solid thud beside her, moaning as if his ill fate was the worst that could happen to a body. Then (as if that were not enough to confirm this day was truly the most miserable of them all) an orange bounced off her head and rolled onto the ground.

"Ouch!" Elena slapped a hand to her russet crown. Ignoring the man's continued groans, she reached over to where the fruit had landed, digging into its flesh with a gripe. "Ammunition indeed. I'll undoubtedly find a goose egg growing in the morning."

"I would be so fortunate to suffer so little," the man said as he sat upright. "I'll surely have bruises from head to toe."

"Serves you right," Elena retorted. She tried to ignore the way jet-black curls framed a strong face with coffee colored eyes that welcomed any onlooker to drown in them. "What kind of decent man does something as foolish as climb trees? Only a thief attempting to take more than his allotted share."

"I am no thief."

"Then why would you not pick the fruit from one of the lower branches?"

"Because I was not as interested in picking oranges as I was hiding from the calculating mothers of hopeful daughters determined to make a fine match with anyone positioned to secure their station."

It took her a moment to fully appreciate the implication made. When she did, she was quick to bow her head. "My apologies, *señor*. I didn't realize you were with the *nobleza*. Please forgive my loose tongue."

"Nonsense. There's nothing to forgive. In fact, I should probably be thanking you for your attempt to guard this sacred tree of forbidden fruit. After all, it is the only one in the entire village – possibly in all of Spain."

A rueful smile tugged at the corner of his mouth and she knew he was teasing her. Well, if that was the way he wished to play, he would soon learn that games were not only for the gentry.

"Oh, I see. You *are* with the royal court… as their *payaso*."

The man laughed and then stuck out his chest with pride. "Indeed. I am not only the jester, but I am the king of them all. Well, maybe not *el rey* himself. There may be one or two humorous sorts who could best me yet. Let us settle with the Count of Jesters. *De acuerdo?*"

"You're a curious man," Elena said, unsure exactly what to make of his unconventional, but jovial ways.

"And you are a shoeless woman," he replied.

Elena glanced down to her feet. Suddenly embarrassed, she pulled them in and they disappeared under her dress. Attempting to demonstrate that she was not bothered by her own unusual manner, she gave a careless shrug. "I wanted to save my slippers."

"And what an exquisite creation it is. May I?" The man reached for the shoe, plucking it up before she could respond. Then he grasped one tired foot from beneath her dusty hem, lifted it up and gently slipped the bejeweled masterpiece over her toes. "There it is. A perfect fit."